Michael Hardcastle w
in Yorkshire. After l
in the Royal Army Educational Corps before
embarking on a career in journalism, working in a number of roles for provincial daily
newspapers from reporter to chief feature
writer.

He has written more than one hundred
children's books since his first was published
in 1966, but still finds time to visit schools
and colleges all over Britain to talk about
books and writing. In 1988 he was awarded
an MBE in recognition of his services to
children's books. He is married and lives in
Beverley, near Hull.

02006

And Davey Must Score

Michael Hardcastle

Goal Kings
BOOK THREE

faber and faber

First published in 1998
by Faber and Faber Limited
3 Queen Square London WC1N 3AU

Typeset by Avon Dataset, Bidford-on-Avon, Warwickshire
Printed and bound in England by Mackays of Chatham PLC,
Chatham, Kent

© Michael Hardcastle, 1998

Michael Hardcastle is hereby identified as author of this work in
accordance with Section 77 of the Copyright, Designs and
Patents Act 1988

A CIP record for this book
is available from the British Library

ISBN 0–571–19365–X

2 4 6 8 10 9 7 5 3 1

Contents

1 On Trial   1

2 Snookered!   18

3 In Trouble   41

4 Walk Out   65

5 Phone In   88

6 Revenge Match   107

7 Early Finish   131

8 A Different Game   148

1 *On Trial*

The man with the spiky grey hair looked hard at Davey and then asked the inevitable question. 'So, where d'you play then?'

'Striker.'

Greg Kingston's eyebrows, so far untouched by grey, shot up. 'Really? I'd've thought you were a bit on the short side for that job. Score any goals for anyone last season?'

Davey swallowed. He knew that League coaches kept in touch with one another, often swapped news items about their own teams and individual players, so Mr Kingston could easily discover the truth if Davey misled him in any way.

'I was with Rodale – you know, the Goal Kings – in the Highlea Sunday League. They've got a top striker in Alex Todd and they also had a foreign player some of the time. But I was the next choice, always played when there was a place in the team.'

'All that's interesting, Davey lad, but you didn't answer my question. How many goals did *you* get?'

'Six. No, that's a lie.' He paused deliberately, hoping the Redville coach would be impressed by honesty. 'It was actually eight. I was thinking perhaps I shouldn't include a couple of tap-ins. Couldn't miss those, really.'

Kingston's cool blue eyes had narrowed. 'First time I've ever heard a real striker *forget* to claim goals when he put the ball in the back of the net however they were scored, thunderbolts or toe-enders.'

Davey shrugged. 'Well, the other guys set them up, all I did was finish it off for them.

'That's the main thing about strikers, being in the right place at the right time.'

'Suppose so,' agreed Davey, pursuing his line in modesty. He wasn't sure, though, that it was what the coach wanted to hear.

'How's your heading? At least your hair won't get in the way!'

Davey laughed, automatically running his hand over his cropped fair hair. 'One of the reasons why I like it as short as this! In fact, I'm a good climber. Scored half of my Kings' goals with my head.'

'OK.' Greg Kingston gave the impression he'd heard enough. 'I'm putting you on in that five-a-side over there. You'll be taking Oliver's place, that boy with the broken nose. He wanted to be a striker but he's not tough enough. Tried boxing and got hit immediately. That's no good. Scorers are like boxers, they've got to duck out of trouble and hit like lightning when they see an opening. Not much else matters if you're going to be a winner.'

'I'll be like that,' Davey promised. 'You watch.'

'Oh, I'll be watching all right, David Stroud. That's my sole purpose in life, finding real talent for Redville Rangers. That's why everyone's here today, to demonstrate they possess the skills I need to sign 'em up for Redville for the new season. It's why I like trials. I'll be watching you, David, *and* all the others. There's no shortage of competition so you've got to be good.'

'I'll prove I am, Mr Kingston. Honest!'

The coach grinned. Then he turned to the furious little game taking place on the multi-pitch beside the tree-lined river bank. 'Ollie!' he yelled in a voice that was like an explosion. 'Time to give it a rest. Your replacement's coming on.'

Ollie couldn't have failed to hear the shout but he wasn't keen to respond. Even when the coach roared a second time Ollie managed to look mystified before, hesitantly, he pointed at himself and enquired: 'You mean me, guv?'

A fierce nod and a beckoning finger were still needed to get him off the pitch. When he moved he tweaked his damaged nose as if to try to restore it to normality.

'Not good at discipline, that boy,' the coach remarked to Davey. 'So don't you follow his example, David.'

'I won't, Mr Kingston,' Davey assured him while getting a very angry stare from the displaced Ollie.

Davey, discarding his track suit and straightening his shorts, sensed that the next few minutes might be vital for his future. If he didn't impress in this pre-season trial then his hoped-for career in football might be a mirage. He believed he had no real hope of making progress with the Goal Kings, the team he'd played for – or, all too often, not played for – over the past two seasons. So this was the time to make a fresh start with a team that would cherish him; and, above all, a team that was going places, going right to the top. In Davey's view, the Goal Kings were going backwards under Ricky Todd's leadership. So, when he'd spotted the advert in the newsagent's that Redville Rangers were looking for players for the new season he'd phoned the quoted number the moment he got home. The coach himself had answered and seemed delighted to hear from him. Davey hadn't heard of Greg Kingston but, of course, he didn't admit that; he claimed that he actually admired the way Redville played, although in truth he'd seen them in action only once and that was just for half a game. However, Mr Kingston wasn't interested in flattery, only whether he was going to get a player who would 'make a meaningful contribution' to his team.

Now the moment had come for Davey to

prove his claims to be the sort of goal-scorer *any* quality team would be desperate to sign. It felt strange to be putting on the glowing red shirt of Redville instead of the purple of the Goal Kings but he hoped he'd soon be used to the change. The coach had also handed him a yellow sash to indicate which of the sides he'd be playing for in the five-a-side. Ollie simply glared at him as they passed on the touch-line but Davey expected that; he himself always felt indignant when a coach took him off before the game was over. If you weren't on the pitch then you couldn't score goals, and goals were all that mattered in his football life.

The playing area marked out for the trial game was about three-quarters of a normal pitch and so there was plenty of opportunity for anyone to run with the ball if he was fast and had good control.

Davey threw himself into action from the moment he received his first pass from a red-haired boy with surprisingly long arms. At once he set off on a mazy run out to the right before cutting inside, swerving past a rather tired tackle and then tried to lob the goalkeeper who was way off his line. The goalie hadn't expected a shot so soon from the attacker and hadn't even started to back-pedal. His luck was in because a light breeze had got up and it carried the ball just wide of the far post.

'Damn!' exploded Davey, glancing at the touch-line to see whether the coach had noted his goal attempt. He surely had but Greg Kingston was neither applauding him nor even looking at him. Perhaps, Davey reflected, he thinks I shot too soon. Yet the early shot was one of his own favourite tactical ploys. Goalkeepers usually expected a striker to close in before shooting. So it was often worth shooting as soon as possible to take the goalie by surprise and so have a better chance of beating him. This time, though, he'd been foiled by something as unpredictable as a gust of wind.

That run and shot had alerted the opposition to some of Davey's skills. Next time he had the ball he didn't keep it more than a split second. His challenger went through him like a bulldozer demolishing a brick wall. Davey, who also got a kick on the inside of his thigh, reacted to the sharp pain by lashing out, swinging his leg round like a scythe to catch the offender's ankle. Of course, the boy made a meal of the incident, falling like a sack of coal, clutching his leg and wailing. The ref, one of the young assistants the coach kept with him for such occasions, waved an admonishing finger at Davey.

'We don't go in for conduct like that at Redville,' he warned. 'Do anything like that again and you'll be sent off, double-quick time.'

'Sorry,' Davey muttered through clenched teeth. He knew how foolish it would be to antagonize anyone connected to the team.

The coach, too, had something to say. 'Don't let yourself be provoked, David. Get on with the game, not the revenge.'

Well, at least he knows my name, Davey comforted himself, even if not quite accurately. But why, he wondered, didn't Mr Kingston criticize the boy who'd brought him down in the first place? Was he one of the coach's favourites? That sort of thing, he believed, was quite normal with most teams.

Alex, for instance, was predictably his father's favourite at Rodale Goal Kings and another who could do no wrong was Josh Rowley, nowadays a central defender but still chosen to play up front from time to time and in emergencies. Josh was quite good at scoring goals at set-pieces and when that happened Davey knew he himself had little chance of claiming a striker's role in the Kings' next match because Josh would be switched to the attack instead.

The incident with the boy who resembled a bulldozer was no longer in his mind when he got his next scoring chance. Once again his red-haired team-mate provided him with a cleverly flicked pass that enabled Davey to dart behind a slow-turning defender and get a clear sight of goal. This time he wasn't going to shoot too soon.

As another defender came towards him Davey slowed down and then, as his opponent hesitated, accelerated; his change of pace with an ability to produce a real burst of speed from almost a standing start was one of his greatest assets. It helped him to fool the uncertain defender and then leave the goalkeeper nonplussed. Davey surged past them both on his diagonal run and then almost casually sidefooted the ball into the unguarded net.

Right arm raised vertically to salute his own achievement, he spun round to see who else was celebrating. Hardly anybody was. His team-mates had turned, smiled and started to trot back to the centre circle. None of them had scored so, in their eyes, there wasn't anything to get excited about. This was a trial and so what mattered was personal, not team, performances. Davey swallowed his disappointment that Mr Kingston wasn't taking any notice of him, either. The coach was deep in conversation with another of his cronies. Had he even *seen* the goal? Davey had no way of knowing. But surely he *must* have done.

Soon he was in the heart of the action again when he picked up a loose ball, turned, twisted, tried to find a way past two dogged opponents and then, after back-heeling the ball, spun round to regain possession. That was the moment he went down, pushed over forcefully by the boy he'd just outwitted. His opponent fell, too, but saved himself by landing on Davey. Then, as he got up, he deliberately crushed his knee into Davey's groin.

The pain was agonizing but no one came to his help as he lay there, doubled up. The ball had been collected by another opponent who raced away, pursued by Davey's teammates and, less speedily, by the ref. Slowly, as the pain began to subside, Davey got to his feet. The action had moved well away from him so he was entirely on his own. He noticed the coach was glancing in his direction and so he tried to overcome his discomfort by running; but that wasn't easy in his present state. By now the ball was in the goalkeeper's hands and he punted it hard upfield towards Davey. He made a great effort to reach it but, unluckily, the bounce beat him and the ball went over his head. Gritting his teeth, Davey turned again and tried to give chase, only to slow down when he saw a defender had possession, a defender too far away for Davey to challenge. His only consolation for missing a chance to take a pass and then run at the defence was that the pain had now almost vanished.

A few minutes later, without Davey getting a touch of the ball again, the ref blew for the end of the match. Davey had no idea what the score was and for all he knew he might be the only scorer. If that was so then he must surely have impressed the Redville coach.

Greg Kingston patted a few players on the shoulder and exchanged comments with them as they grouped round him before he sent them off to change. Davey hung back, waiting to hear the coach's verdict on his performance. Greg Kingston looked at him as if making sure he'd remember his face. Then he asked, 'So how d'you think you performed out there, David?'

It wasn't what Davey had been expecting. Coaches usually delivered opinions instead of wanting to hear someone else's. Unsure how to reply he paused before saying cautiously, 'OK, I suppose. I mean, I got a goal, didn't I? But I didn't get much support.'

As soon as he'd said the last few words he wished he hadn't. Very probably the coach didn't want to hear criticism of players in his squad. Still, Davey felt it was true so his honesty might be appreciated.

'Anything you should have done, *could* have done, to improve your play?' Mr Kingston enquired next, still revealing nothing whatsoever of his feelings.

'Er, I don't really know. I mean, I always run about a lot, like to keep on the move, get into positions to receive the ball from a team-mate or pick up any rebounds. You know, that sort of thing. Oh, and I'm always ready to take on opponents. I usually feel confident when I'm running at defenders.'

At school he'd been told that was one of his strengths, he wasn't easily intimidated however strong the opposition. He wasn't sure that Ricky Todd at Rodale believed it but then Mr Todd rarely had anything favourable to say about him.

The coach was nodding. 'Yes, I think most of that's true. But you're ignoring the main question: what did you fail to do? What *should* you have done? You see, I like to hear a player work out his own shortcomings. If you can do that for yourself you're more likely to correct things at the earliest opportunity. Too often players promptly forget what a coach tells 'em.'

Davey cast about in his mind, trying feverishly to come up with something he'd failed in; all too clearly, the Redville coach had seen something important. Davey sensed that if he could identify it, admit to it, there was a chance Mr Kingston would sign him on.

'Sorry,' he said at last. 'Just can't think of anything, Mr Kingston.'

'Pity,' said the coach sharply. 'I hoped you'd see that after you've been knocked down in a tackle you should get up right away and get on with the task of *playing*. Lying around in a sulk is no good to anyone.'

'But I didn't!' Davey protested. 'I was in agony. That guy just kneed me in the bal – sorry, the groin. Did it on purpose, I'm sure. Honestly, Boss, I was in agony. No way I could have run around straight afterwards.'

The coach was shaking his head as if in sorrow. 'David, this is a tough old game, so you have to be tough to play it. If things go wrong you've just got to get on with it, you can't roll around looking for sympathy. Because that's what it seemed to me you were doing. Pain is a funny thing. Some people give in to it, others do their best to ignore it.

If you're really fired up for a game then usually, *usually*, you can cope with troubles like a knock on the knee or a kick in a tender place. You *have* to, if you want to be a winner.'

Davey didn't know what to say. It was obvious the coach thought he wasn't brave enough to overcome real pain. Only he himself knew he hadn't been putting it on, that he really had been suffering too much to continue immediately (and it was still painful when he touched himself down there so that proved to him it had been a severe blow).

'Next time,' he said to break the silence, 'next time I'll get up immediately and try to forget it. Honestly, I'm not a wimp, or timid. But, you see –'

'Next time, well, I don't know when that's going to be, David,' the coach cut in. 'I don't think you're quite ready for Redville at the moment. Maybe I could judge better after seeing you in a normal competitive match but that's not possible with the new season just about to start. No, I'll just have to see how things go. If a chance comes up to give you a game, well, I'll certainly let you know.'

Davey felt like saying something

unforgivable but managed not to; after all, Redville were almost a local team and very likely he'd meet Greg Kingston on another occasion. All the same, it was plain he had no future with his team.

'So, David, thanks for turning up for the trial,' Kingston smiled, holding out his hand for a civil parting. 'I wish you luck in the future. Just remember this: all top players have to force themselves through the pain barrier at times. And that's why they *are* at the top.'

'Thanks,' said Davey. He was turning away when he remembered something. 'Oh, by the way, I'm not David. My name's *Davey*, Davey Stroud.'

'Oh, right. Sorry I got it wrong. Bye, Davey.'

As he trudged along the riverside path towards the place where he could catch the next bus he reflected on his parting comment to the coach. He didn't doubt that he'd be remembered, but probably for the wrong reasons. Still, he didn't regret his words: he was tired of being trampled on by just about everybody. Davey *knew* he had talent, *knew* that he could score goals at any level of football, *knew* he only needed to be given an extended run in a team to prove it. If only he could *find* such a team . . .

As usual, there wasn't a bus when you wanted one. Davey leaned against the side of the shelter and launched himself into one of his favourite routines: imitating a radio commentator describing one of his goals. 'And now the goalkeeper's creeping off his line, trying to judge the moment to jump for the cross that must be coming. And here it comes – and the goalie's MISSED it – missed it completely. A defender tries to hack it clear – and he misses it, too. Now Davey Stroud is coming on to it like a starving wolf – and Davey must score! And he does! And that's Davey's third goal for England and the match is only thirty minutes old. What a player!'

Davey sighed, opened his eyes and saw that there was still no sign of an approaching bus.

2 Snookered!

Ricky Todd took a long look down his cue at the red lying on the top cushion because it was his best option. Carefully he took aim and, to his joy, struck it perfectly, the red clinging to the cushion all the way until it disappeared into the corner pocket.

'Another fluke!' his son snapped in exasperation. 'Honestly, I've no chance against that sort of thing.'

'No fluke at all,' Ricky told him quietly as he sized up a chance of a colour. Blue looked the most promising prospect. 'If you make sure the cue ball hits the cushion at the same instant it strikes the object ball, well, that ball will stay on the cushion, won't fall away. And that's just what I managed.'

The blue, however, didn't fall into the middle bag as he'd hoped. On the other hand, the cue ball trickled behind the brown to leave Alex completely snookered on his next shot. His father grinned and mouthed an apology.

'That's just typical, you get all the luck going!' Alex fumed. 'How'm I going to get to the last red from behind the brown?'

'Work it out,' his father was about to say when, impetuously, Alex sent the cue ball chasing desperately round the table before it finally collided with the pink to provide his opponent with six extra points.

'Alex, I told you, you could have worked out the angles first before whacking the ball like that. It was perfectly possible to reach the red if you'd used your brain. I've been thinking, your snooker's like your football: you're just reacting to situations instead of making an intelligent assessment of what's the best thing you can do. Then –'

'No, that's rubbish!' Alex interrupted. 'The two games are completely different, one's slow and one's fast. You can take your time over snooker, take *ages* if you want, before making a shot. At soccer you've got to do what comes straight into your head when you're on the ball. So –'

'*Exactly* what I'm saying to you,' Ricky replied, still in a mild tone. 'If you're really on the ball at soccer then you can anticipate what could happen when someone else has possession. You take up a good position for a pass or a clearance. Then you'll have time, maybe plenty of time, to decide what to do with the ball, how to make the most of an opening. You'll have seen where defenders are and who's left-footed and who can kick only with the right. That way you'll make a bigger contribution to the team's effort.'

Alex had been impatiently twirling his cue between his fingers, really waiting only for his dad to make his next shot and finish the game as soon as possible. Even though he'd been given three blacks' (21 points) start he knew he'd never really stood a chance of winning. But he'd never admit that lack of confidence to anyone.

'You make soccer sound like a chess match,' he muttered. 'You can't work it all out in advance. If you're really skilful on the ball you'll do OK whatever the other team's up to. And you know I'm the best striker around.

That's why I should captain the Kings. Dad, you've got to give me the captaincy this season. I deserve it.'

'Alex, I don't have to do any such thing. You know how people reacted last season when the subject cropped up. I can't be seen to be favouring you simply because you're my son. I always try to ensure that everyone is treated the same. That's the way it's got to be in a team, otherwise you're in trouble because jealousies flare up and some boys might even seek revenge for the slights they think they've suffered.' He ran his fingers through his wavy chestnut hair. 'Look, I don't want to talk about this any more. Danny is a brilliant player, he's sensible and fair-minded, he'll always do a good job for us.'

'But he's a *goalkeeper*! Goalies are no good as captains, they're too far from the real action, most of the time. He can't see what's going on in the middle when there's a scrap or somebody's injured.'

'Alex, we do have a coach as well as a captain, remember. Tactics and dealing with on-the-pitch incidents is my job. The skipper's there to lift morale, lead by example, that sort of thing. Oh, and tossing-up for choice of ends!'

Alex wasn't going to be deflected by attempts at humour. 'Listen, Dad, I know he's your favourite player – well, one of them along with Josh and Dominic – oh, and Joe, I suppose. But you're ignoring me because I'm your son. You look after everybody else but you ignore me so nobody can accuse you of favouritism. Well, *that's* not fair. I'm the one losing out.'

'Look, Alex, I really didn't want to say this but I've got to be honest,' Ricky said gently. 'I don't think you're improving as a player, as a team player, I mean. No, listen, please. If I don't spell this out I'm not being fair to anyone. I have to assess you in exactly the same way as any other Kings' player. No one is guaranteed a place in our line-up for every match, not even you. Just because I'm the coach you can't expect to play if you're not performing. If one of my salesmen at the furniture factory consistently fails to meet his quotas then I have to let him go. The same applies to you.'

The expected explosion wasn't forthcoming. Alex folded his bottom lip under his teeth and then flicked back the hair above his right eyebrow. For several moments he didn't say so much as a single word.

'You're saying you're going to drop me, aren't you?' he said eventually, still surprisingly calm.

'I may have to,' his father answered in the same matter-of-fact manner. 'Look, Alex, the Kings had a poor time last season, everyone recognizes that. We won nothing and even finished in the bottom half of the League table. Big difference from the previous season when we won the Knock-out Cup and –'

'Yeah, and that was under a different coach, wasn't it? Sam Saxton,' Alex pointed out spitefully. That was a way of hitting back at what he considered his dad's disloyalty.

'Thank you for reminding me of that. I can tell you I hadn't forgotten it. And it helps to make my point. You say you're being judged by me and that's true. But I'm being judged by every Kings' player and supporter and parent. Yes, especially the parents. If our results aren't good in the new season they'll be calling for my head. Then there were all sorts of rumours at the end of last season about people like Clark Kelly and Steve Parbold who might fancy coaching.'

Alex was shaking his head. 'Dad, you've nothing to worry about, honestly. I mean, when do we ever see those guys at our matches? Only when it's something special. *Mrs* Kelly and *Mrs* Parbold, yes, they turn up.'

'Well I honestly think, Alex, that it might be best if I rested you for the first couple of matches. Just to see how we get on with a different formation.'

'I *knew* it,' Alex muttered with a bitterness his father hadn't heard for a long time. 'You've been got at by Davey and Josh and that crowd. They've always wanted to be top striker. Dad, how could you?'

This wasn't entirely the reaction Ricky had expected but he thought he knew the reason for Alex's failure to explode in familiar fashion when events went against him. He'd been waiting for a good opportunity to raise the matter and this evening's visit to the Rodale Club to play snooker seemed to be it. 'Look, Alex, there are times when things simply don't work out as you want them to. I thought it'd be perfectly OK for me to coach the Kings when you were playing for them. You thought so, too, I know.

'But for some reason I can't put my finger on, it isn't working. You're not playing as well as you did before I took over. Maybe I'm not able to bring the best out of you just because you *are* my son. Maybe I'm not as impartial as I want to be, *need* to be. I'm not happy about the situation and you aren't, are you?'

'Doesn't bother me,' Alex said unconvincingly.

'Doesn't it? I think it does. Isn't that why you were asking the Torridon coach if he had a vacancy for a striker this season?'

Alex's eyes had rarely opened so wide. 'Who told you that? I never did! I only want to play for the Kings.'

'Son, this is still a village, you know. In villages everybody, or just about everybody, knows everyone else. People gossip, tell each other titbits of news and rumour. The whole village knows about the Kings so, naturally, you and me and the rest of the players are of interest to a lot of people. So when you start chatting up an opposition coach somebody's going to mention it to someone else and that someone else will tell *me*.'

Alex, still trying to come to terms with this revelation, was shaking his head non-stop. 'It wasn't like that, I haven't been chatting up anyone. I mean, he spoke to me first, honest, Dad. Just said it must be a bit tricky playing for a team your dad was coaching. I suppose he was being friendly after the game. You know, after we played Torridon last time and beat 'em 3–2. That was when Davey got two lucky goals I set up for him.'

Ricky nodded. 'So what did you say? Did you agree with him?'

Alex flicked his hair back again and his father noticed the pinkness in his cheeks. 'Er, I might've done. Can't remember exactly. He remembered me because I got the winner. So –'

'But that was from the penalty spot,' his father pointed out. 'The most memorable thing about that match was that we came so darned close to losing it after being streets ahead of them. Alex, I want the truth: did you start this conversation or did he? No half-truths, I want to know exactly what happened.'

Alex was brushing his eyebrows in a vigorous manner, a mannerism Ricky believed indicated that Alex wasn't at all sure of himself. In fact, it was really Alex's way of trying to give the impression he was in the right whatever he said or did. 'I told you, he started it, said he thought I'd played well. That I was just the sort of player he needed in *his* side. I create chances, he said that. I had to agree with him, didn't I? Because it's true.'

'Sometimes you do, sometimes you don't,' Ricky replied casually. 'OK, I accept your version. But I want you to be equally truthful about this question: have you spoken to him again since then?'

'Look, I don't want to talk about this, it's totally unimportant,' Alex replied, twirling his cue again. 'I thought we were supposed to be playing snooker. It's your shot, Dad.'

'Alex, you must know perfectly well I'm not going to drop this subject until I've got the truth. You know I'm a great believer in loyalty, loyalty within my family, my factory,

my football team, everywhere. So if somebody I care about is guilty of disloyalty I need
to know *why*. Just tell me what's going on,'
Ricky demanded.

'How d'you know *anything's* going on?'
Alex persisted sullenly.

'Oh, Alex, use your brains! Joe Parbold's
dad works at the building society – and so
does Dane Credland, your friendly Torridon
coach. Well, when men get together and talk
about football it's obvious they'll gossip
about people they know. In this case, me and
you. Apparently Dane was interested in
finding out from Steve Parbold whether it
was true that you wanted to get away from
the Kings – and from me. Does that answer
your question about *how* I know something's
going on?'

'Suppose so,' Alex conceded. 'But he was
interested in me, I wasn't trying to get away
from the Kings. But – but – if you're thinking
of dropping me I have to have somewhere to
go, haven't I?'

'Did he actually offer you a chance to sign
for Torridon? Did he say he'd like to sign you
up?'

As if suddenly tired of standing up Alex sank into the black leather sofa at the side of the room under the scoreboard. The movement gave him a moment to decide how to answer. 'Yeah,' he announced positively, 'he did. He said I was just the sort of player he was looking for and he'd guarantee me a place in the team every week.'

His dad frowned in disbelief. 'Alex, is that the truth? He actually said you'd be in the team every week without fail?'

'That's what he said,' Alex confirmed. 'I told you, I didn't ask him for it. He just thinks I've a great future as a striker.' He paused and then added, 'And you don't, do you, Dad? You've just said you think I've lost it, gone backwards, something like that.'

'So what was your answer?'

Alex hesitated again. 'I said I'd think about it. I mean, you *know* the Kings are my best team but I need to score goals. And the other guys in our team aren't always, well, up to my standard, are they? *You* keep saying we're not making the progress we should. So if you're going to drop me I might as well sign for somebody else. The Dons aren't that bad.

If I hadn't scored the penalty to put us three-up in the Cup-tie they could've beaten us. They played some good stuff in the second half, didn't they, when they grabbed two goals?'

Ricky picked up his cue again but didn't approach the table. Alex couldn't imagine what his dad was going to say next. Eventually, he turned and said quietly, 'Alex, I don't want to dash your hopes over this but it could just be that Dane Credland is trying to wind me up. He's young, very young, so young-looking I wasn't even sure he was old enough to have left school and gone to work until I heard he was at the building society. So he's very inexperienced as a coach. But that doesn't prevent him from thinking he can wind me up by trying to tempt my son away from the Kings. Very likely he'd regard that as a neat trick, an ace.'

Alex sat up straight. 'You mean he doesn't really want me? He's only talking about signing me to get at you? I don't believe it!'

'You don't have to. But at all levels of football there are people ready to pull a fast one or try some bit of cunning to win a particular advantage. It happens in business as well as in football. I could be wrong, but that's the feeling I have.'

'But Dane's got lots of bright ideas, he really wants Torridon to go right to the top. And he's giving me that guarantee, remember.'

'Ah, so it's "Dane" now, is it? Obviously you know him well enough to be on those sort of terms, Alex. Well, if that's what you want, I'm not going to stop you. If loyalty counts for nothing I'm sorry, but I'm not going to stop you getting what you want. I believe in freedom, in an individual choosing for himself. That's the way I run my own business.'

Alex flicked his hair back again. 'So you're letting me go, right? You don't care if I leave the Kings?'

'Son, it's *your* choice. I've just pointed that out. You've already said you've got this guarantee of a permanent place in their team. I can't give the same guarantee about the Kings. I'll be sorry to see you playing for someone else but if it's what you want, then OK, that's how it's got to be.'

Alex swung towards him and asked fiercely, 'So who're you going to put in my place? Go on, tell me who's better?'

'That's not the way to look at it and you know it,' Ricky said, sounding exasperated. 'Some people play at their best because they're in tune with their partner, their fellow strikers. Others play out of their skin because they regard the other striker as a rival. I mean, you're a bit like that. But it's too soon to tell what I'm going to do. The season's barely started, we haven't even played our first League game yet. Only that miserable five-a-side knock-out thing. I've just got to try a few permutations, see what clicks.'

'It's Josh you want up there, isn't it?' Alex persisted.

'No. You know as well as I do that Josh has fitted in really well at the back. Converting him to a back-four player was one of my successes of last season.' He paused and then said softly, 'Some might say my *only* success. Anyway, Josh is happy in defence. If he scores when he comes up for set-pieces that's a bonus. After all, his extra height is always going to be a help wherever he plays.'

Alex was prowling round the table, moodily aiming his cue at various colours but not actually striking them. Ricky wished he could offer him some comforting words but experience told him that Alex wouldn't listen. Once he'd made his mind up about a course of action hardly anything deflected him. That was a situation that applied equally to himself, Ricky knew.

'Look, let's pack –' he was saying when Alex jumped to another conclusion.

'I know, you're going to put Davey and Gareth together! But that'd be crazy. Davey's useless in the air, he never heads anything. There isn't a striker in the world as small as him. He's a joke.'

'Alex, stop this! Have you lost all sense of judgement? You know very well that's not true. Young Davey is –'

'– *young* Davey? Why d'you call him that? He's exactly the same age as me, has to be to be in our League.'

'Alex, calm down, please. We should never have got into this sort of discussion in the first place. I know how you feel but you've got to recognize that *I* am the coach and I run the team in the best interests of everybody, not just for the benefit of one or two special players. Or for you, just because we're related. I've told you all this before and this is the very last time we're going to rake over the same ground.' He took a breath but for once Alex wasn't inclined to interrupt. 'Davey *is* small but he can jump. In fact, he jumps very well indeed, seems to have that valuable trick of being able to hang in the air for a split second to make sure he gets a good contact on a header. He's a one-hundred-per-cent trier with good positional sense. *That's* why he deserves an extended run in the team.

'Oh yes, and Gareth,' he went on when Alex remained silent. 'Well, I think he's got real potential up front. After all, he scored that spectacular scissors-kick goal in our last match and —'

'It was a complete fluke! Gareth himself admits it. Didn't even know where the net was when he got his boot to it.'

'Well, maybe, but the point is he was in the right place at the right moment. It's where you should have been, Alex. Don't you agree?

I mean, I'd've been thrilled, *thrilled*, if you'd scored a goal like that.'

'I can score better goals than that,' Alex muttered. 'But if you're going to *drop* me I might as well go somewhere else.'

Ricky's patience had run out. 'Alex, in this life you've got to fight for what you want, not moan,' he said crisply, snapping his cue back into the rack, the signal that their game was finished. 'I've fought for the things I wanted and got them. When I wanted to marry your mother she was already engaged to someone else but I didn't let that stop me. You've heard that story several times. When I wanted my own furniture factory, my own business, I had to battle against the odds to get it. Now I might have to fight just as hard to keep it. That's –'

'What's all that about? You haven't said anything about that before, Dad.'

'No, and I'm not saying anything about it now. It's too soon. All I'm saying is that in business you're always battling against something, or somebody. Football's the same, you have to battle for what you want. If you want to keep playing for the Kings, Alex, then fight for your place, prove to me you're the best striker we've got. OK?'

'I shouldn't have to prove anything,' the dark-haired boy said truculently. 'You should know I'm the best.'

Ricky was already on his way out of the room. At the door he turned and said, 'If you want a lift home you're welcome to it. If you prefer to walk, that's fine.'

'I'm going to see Matthew,' Alex announced. 'At least I can talk to him about real football, not some kind of fantasy!'

'Please yourself,' Ricky told him and headed for the car-park.

Ricky hadn't been home five minutes when the phone rang. Grimacing because he'd have preferred a quiet drink in front of the TV, he picked up the receiver. He feared it would be about his factory but it turned out to be Jane Allenby, unofficially his assistant coach with the Kings and mother of Dominic, one of the team's outstanding defenders.

'I've got some excellent news, Ricky,' she told him.

'I could do with it. Not been a good day today.'

'Oh, nothing serious, I hope.'

'Nothing I can talk about. Oh, apart from Alex, who's in his surliest mood. I had to tell him he's not an automatic choice at present. Hoped that might fire him up, make him realize he has to show more spirit and determination. But he seems to think he's entitled to a place in the team whatever his form. I told him that's not on.'

There was a pause before Jane answered as if she were striving for a diplomatic comment. Then she realized that the news she had might help to solve the problem with Alex. 'Ricky, do you remember that when we played Stonecreek Pirates they had a very talented fair-haired player called Reuben Jones? A left-sided player, wonderfully accurate passer with his left foot.'

'Er, yes,' he agreed, although he couldn't immediately bring the player to mind. What he could recall was that the Kings collectively hadn't played very well in a drawn game against an inferior team.

'I thought you would,' Jane replied, wondering what was troubling Ricky because he wasn't his usual alert self. 'Well, he's free to sign for us if we want him. *If*! I'm sure he'd make a terrific difference to us. He'd supply the ammunition the strikers would fire. Alex would get the kind of service from midfield he must dream about. So, what d'you think, Ricky?'

'Well, yes, I'm interested. Quality players at this level aren't readily available, we all know that,' he replied, still sounding cautious. 'But are you absolutely sure he's a free agent? That Stonecreek haven't got his registration for the new season?'

'Definitely! That was the first thing I checked up on. I've heard about the trouble a club can get into if they try to sign up another club's player. The thing is, Reuben's not happy with the Pirates' coach and it's probably mutual. Something to do with a difference over tactics and roles. At the moment he doesn't want to say too much about it. He's simply adamant he's not re-signing for the Pirates. He'd be happy to come to us. He said he thought we weren't a bad side last season! Fair comment, I suppose. Oh, and he's also having a bit of a hard time at home at present. His mum had yet another baby recently and the house really is a bit crowded. That's how I met Reuben – I was his mum's midwife.'

'Not in any trouble, is he? I mean, could that be the reason he wants a change of team?'

She hesitated. 'I doubt it. I think I'm a reasonable judge of character and that I could tell when I'm being manipulated. Also, I was the one who started the chat about football. Found myself on my own with him for a few moments while his mum was in the bathroom. So I asked about his interests. Soon as he mentioned football I remembered where I'd seen him before. He has that very fair hair, almost white, really. And then –'

'Right, right,' Ricky cut in. He was beginning to resent the length of time this call was taking. 'Does Dominic have an opinion about this boy? Does he remember him?'

'Oh, I haven't said a word to Dominic about this, Ricky. I regard it as totally confidential until we're in a position to decide what to do about Reuben. Basically, it will be your decision, won't it? Your word is final because you're the coach.'

'True. OK. Well, thanks, Jane. Very good of

you to go to all this trouble. So let's see how he shapes up at Tuesday evening's training session. I'll invite him along – or you could as you've got his home details. We'll take it from there. How's that?'

'Fine. I'll do that. D'you know, Ricky, I have a gut feeling that Reuben Jones is going to make a real difference to the Kings and our future.'

Foggy, who got his name because of the foghorn-loudness of his voice, could probably be heard well beyond the confines of the Rodale Kings' dressing-room. In his present exuberant mood, however, he didn't mind if the whole world heard him.

'Just you keep pinging in the passes and crosses, Rube mate, and I'll do the rest,' he promised extravagantly. 'Shouldn't be surprised if I don't get a hat-trick today. So make sure you deliver, Rube.'

Reuben Jones, sitting bare-legged beside his new captain, Danny Loxham, winced. 'If you don't mind, I like my name in full. Don't like it shortened in any way. Don't like Jonesy, either. I'm *Reuben*, all right?'

'Suit yourself, mate. I like being Foggy. Nobody ever forgets me or my name. And after today's goal spree I'll be known as King

41

Foggy! Hey, how about that, fellas? Great, isn't it?'

Alex, slumped against the far wall, was seething, muttering under his breath, 'Just shut up, shut up, shut up!' He had every reason to feel aggrieved, he believed, for he would be on the subs' bench with Davey Stroud while Foggy pranced about up front with none other than Josh Rowley. In his eyes, the situation couldn't have been worse: he was being replaced by a non-striker and an ex-striker. He wasn't even sure that he should regard Josh as ever having been a real striker at any time. Foggy, in Alex's view, was just a pain in the neck, forever strutting around and claiming to be the best at everything. In reality Foggy did have pace and he certainly worked at his game, practising regularly and training diligently. His main weapon, of course, was confidence and he still couldn't understand why Danny Loxham, the goalkeeper, had been preferred ahead of him as the captain of the Kings.

Josh had the distinct advantage of being the tallest boy in the team, at least a head higher than anyone else, and he'd become a winner in the air whether in attack or defence. That was why he was always sent up into the box for corners and free kicks and his record of headed goals was impressive. But, in Alex's eyes, Josh hadn't anything like the same skills on the ground and he certainly lacked the real striker's instinct for being in the right place at the right moment to snatch a goal. Alex was ignoring his father's comment that Alex himself seemed to have lost that knack in his own play.

'Listen, just play your own game, Reuben,' Danny advised the newcomer in a tone little above a whisper. 'Foggy winds everybody up when he gets the chance. Must say, I never thought he'd be picked as an all-out striker but the Boss seems to want to change everything at present. Suppose that's natural at the start of a new season. Just hope he's happy with me in goal. But you never know!'

The Boss chose that moment to walk in and the effect on every player was instantaneous. Alex, however, was the only one who deliberately avoided his eye. He and his dad had nothing to say to each other: unless, that is, Ricky had changed his mind and restored him to the team as first choice striker.

'Right, boys, I don't have a lot to say because we've talked through most of the main points in training,' Ricky said, standing in the middle of the room, arms folded tightly as if he were hugging himself. 'You all know how vital it is to win our first League game of the season. That's why we're trying a new formation. We need height and pace up front and I'm sure Josh and Foggy will provide it. We've got to attack and attack and with two strikers on the bench we have the reinforcements if we need them.'

Davey glanced across at Alex to see his reaction but Alex, staring woodenly at the floor, was giving nothing away. Davey felt as sick about the changes as Alex but all he could do was hope his chance would come, and come soon.

'You all know how pleased I am that Reuben has joined us and I'm sure he's going to enjoy playing football with the Kings,' Ricky went on, smiling at the fair-haired midfielder whose own expression, however, didn't alter. 'Reuben, if you can manufacture the bullets that our strikers can fire into the opposition's net then everyone will be thankful I found you and persuaded you to become a King!'

This time the most significant look exchanged between players was that involving Dominic Allenby and Joe Parbold. Dominic's eyebrows shot up at their coach's mention of 'his' find but he didn't say a word. Joe, sometimes known as Rocky because of his defensive strengths in the back-four, had heard Dom's account of how his mum had met Reuben Jones but Joe didn't say much at any time and he certainly wasn't going to comment now. His own role in the team wasn't really affected by Reuben's arrival but he'd have to get used to having someone else alongside him in defence in place of Josh.

'Kellington, as I've told you, aren't the toughest opposition we could've faced for our opening match but we've got to treat them as if they were,' Ricky was saying. 'If we can pile on the goals, let's do it. Let's give our supporters a game to remember. It's two years since we won the Knock-out Cup. Time we won something again. And the best trophy would be the League title. That's our real aim.

'From what I've seen, plenty of people are turning up. Some of them will never have seen us, so let's show them we're THE team to support in the Highlea Sunday League. A few may be parents, some of them *your* parents, so I want us to be on our best behaviour. No bad language – never mind the words *other* people use in your hearing! No arguing with the ref, no abusing other players. I don't want any red or yellow cards for indiscipline. In short, I want us to be perfect!'

He paused for effect but, apart from a couple of grins, his players didn't react to that impossible ambition. So the coach didn't need to delay his final instruction, 'Kings, go out and rule!'

Perfection was the word that could certainly be applied to his timing for at that moment the ref poked his head round the dressing-room door and announced cheerfully, 'Time to play, you Rodale Goal Kings, so let's see you on the pitch.'

In contrast to the Goal Kings' traditional

46

colours of purple with white trim, Kellington were in shades of green with green and white hooped socks, a new strip for them which one of their wealthy sponsors had declared was 'bound to be lucky'. The launch of the new season on a sunny but fitfully windy day had encouraged a mini convoy of supporters' cars to accompany the team to Rodale Kings.

Naturally, the home supporters outnumbered the opposition fans and the Kings were greeted by a sustained burst of cheering. Ricky had sent out a message to local inhabitants to 'get behind our team and help make it the most successful in the county – and then the country!' As a businessman he'd long believed in the value of advertising and he felt the team would respond to lots of vocal encouragement at their matches. On one occasion he'd even hired an open-top bus for the team to travel on through and round the village before an important Cup game. Inevitably there were some critics who took the view that the stunt was 'well over the top' but it worked because the team got plenty of publicity and won the Cup-tie.

Alex had decided that as he was merely a

sub he'd miss out on the pre-kick-off kick-in but as he was trotting towards the bench he spotted that Jane Allenby was already standing there. Ricky didn't allow his assistant coach to be in the dressing-room for his talks or post-mortems although most of the players wouldn't have minded her presence. (Dominic was one who might have objected but then he'd have preferred it if she wasn't at any of their matches in any capacity.) Of course, she was welcome when any player took a knock and needed attention because she was usually the only person present with medical skills.

So now Alex curved back towards the pitch and, as he did so, a loose ball came bouncing straight at him. Without hesitation he took a quick sighting of goal, swung his right foot and sent the ball like a projectile into the roof of the net. That unexpected 'goal' gave him an immense fillip, especially as some supporters, unaware that he was a sub for this match, cheered mightily and one called out, 'And make sure you score a few more like that when the match begins, Alex!' It had to be a good omen, Alex decided. As he'd had no further contact with the Torridon coach he was still officially a Kings' player and he was prepared to accept that situation – for the time being.

Ricky, who was chatting to his opposite number, the Kellington coach, on the far touch-line gave no sign he'd witnessed Alex's firecracker of a shot. Then he moved on for a word with a small group of Rodale supporters who included Serena Colmer, Lloyd's mum, and Jakki and Clark Kelly whose son Kieren was one of the pillars of the team's defence. Clark's presence surprised Ricky because usually only Jakki showed a keen interest in the Kings' progress. Ricky made a point of saying something complimentary about Lloyd's contribution in training sessions. In fact, Lloyd was as inconsistent as he was talented and Ricky was forever reviewing his place in the team. Serena, however, believed that Lloyd only played poorly when he was 'put under pressure' to curb his natural free-running style and play strictly to the coach's orders for the benefit of the entire team. On a couple of occasions she'd told Ricky that he wasn't being fair to the boy, that Lloyd wasn't being allowed to 'express himself'.

When the ref summoned the captains to the centre circle for the toss-up, Alex sauntered to the bench. He was thankful that the good weather meant he didn't have to gather up any discarded track-suit tops, a job that made him feel like a waiter in a restaurant.

'How're you feeling, Alex?' Mrs Allenby asked brightly.

'Bad.'

'Pardon?' She was genuinely startled.

'How d'you think I'm feeling when I've been dropped for the first game of the season?'

'Well, if you get on to the pitch later you'll have your chance to prove you should start the next match. That's what subs do, Alex.'

'Not me,' he replied bitterly. 'Dad doesn't rate me these days so I've no chance of getting a game. He's even using a full-back as a striker! I've got the message all right.'

Davey, already sitting on the bench, gave Alex a quick glance but didn't speak. He wondered whether it was true that Alex had fallen completely out of favour with Mr Todd.

If so then his own chances of playing were greatly improved. Davey suddenly felt more cheerful.

Minutes later it was almost impossible for him not to feel slightly more elated. In their first attack, the Goal Kings won a corner on the right when Lloyd, trying to turn an opponent close to the byline, was foiled only because the defender panicked and pushed the ball over the line. Matthew Forrest was renowned for the accuracy of his place kicks and that skill was in evidence immediately as the back-four defender picked out the towering Josh. Kellington must have known he'd be the likely target but no one could reach his altitude as Josh powered in for a header with the goal seemingly at his mercy. Josh's accuracy, however, wasn't within a metre of Tree Forrest's and the ball zoomed harmlessly above the bar.

While Davey couldn't help feeling that a real striker like himself would never have missed such a good chance the coach simply flung his arms upwards in despair. That opening had been the perfect culmination of all their training-ground planning. Everything had gone precisely as he'd hoped, *everything* except the woefulness of the header. A goal within the first three minutes would have been the dream start; if, as he believed, Kellington were a fairly mediocre side then such a setback might have paralysed them, allowing the Kings to score a hatful and send a message to the rest of the League that the Kings were really going to live up to their name this season.

'Great corner, Tree,' Josh clapped with his hands above his head as he jogged back towards the centre. 'I'll convert the next, no danger.'

But he didn't. When the Kings were awarded a free kick on the edge of the box because of a clumsy tackle, Tree's work was squandered again as Josh tried a looping flick of a header that sent the ball metres wide of the upright. 'Come on, Josh, get your act together!' Ricky yelled. He wasn't normally given to voicing criticisms of individual players in such a public manner. Josh's mother, Karen Rowley, standing quite close by, threw him a sharp glance.

Josh himself raised a hand to show he'd

heard and mouthed 'Sorry!' to his coach. Usually Josh wore contact lenses and it occurred to Ricky that perhaps the boy had forgotten them today, though that hardly seemed likely. So, had one dropped out when he missed his first goal attempt?

It didn't look like it. For soon Josh was in action at the other end of the pitch. Cheered by those early let-offs, Kellington confidently strode forward to launch their own attacks. Perhaps, they reasoned, the Goal Kings weren't nearly as good as they'd feared; maybe they'd changed their formation or style and lost shape. Whichever it was, they looked beatable. Tree, who lacked pace, was easily turned by a nippy winger who then cut inside, heading for goal. Lloyd, loitering in midfield without much sense of purpose, was quickly bypassed and the winger then hit a long, powerful crossfield pass. It was a sophisticated bit of play and even the normally astute Dominic Allenby failed to read it. As he hesitated the bounce of the ball beat him and an inrushing attacker gained possession. Hurriedly, the Kings' defence retreated. Danny watched in rising concern from his goalmouth. 'Pick him up, Rocky, pick him up!' he yelled.

Joe Parbold dutifully slid in for a tackle but his timing, too, was at fault. He missed both ball and opponent. Gratefully, the Kellington raider raced on. Now the fast winger was sweeping in for the anticipated pass and the chance of a goal. When he called for the ball he got it, and it was beautifully delivered. Unhesitatingly the winger, with only the goalkeeper to face, shot for goal.

Danny had come off his line and the ball was flying over his head. But, with a remarkable jump from a standing position, he just managed to get a hand to the ball and divert it with the tips of his fingers. Even so, the ball was still looping towards the net and there was nothing the goalie could do to keep it out. Like the famed Seventh Cavalry, however, Josh was galloping to the rescue. It was his anticipation rather than his pace that enabled him to reach the ball with his right leg at full stretch and his toe managed to nudge it wide of the far post. It had been a very near thing and Danny made a point of slapping his team-mate on the shoulder, though he had to reach upwards to do so.

The corner kick came to nothing for, once again, it was Josh who reached the ball and headed it to safety. Ricky, pacing up and down the touch-line apparently lost in his own thoughts, was in a quandary. Should he order Josh to return to the front line where he was supposed to be playing or should he make a tactical switch and send the gangling striker back to his old role in defence? After all, he couldn't spend the entire match rushing from goal-mouth to goal-mouth. Josh's mum had once pointed out to the coach that Josh shouldn't be asked to do too much because 'he's still growing and he seems to have outgrown his strength already'. Ricky wasn't sure how much truth there was in that and when he'd asked Jane, the medical expert, she'd just shrugged and said each boy was different. Above all, though, the Kings needed an attacking force. If the partnership between Josh and Foggy wasn't working then he must do something about it. As he glanced round his eye fell on Davey, sitting on the bench, calmly waiting to enter the action.

Before he could speak to the sub, however,

there was an anguished cry from Foggy, 'I have no one to pass to! I can't do it all on my own!'

Because it was Foggy everyone heard the complaint. Some spectators laughed while others, sporting Kellington's green-and-white colours, jeered or yelled attempted witticisms. Foggy had received the ball from Reuben, the pass being as perfect as he could've hoped for, but when he found himself boxed in by eager opponents he could see no one to help him out; and even Foggy recognized sometimes he couldn't play without the support of team-mates.

Ricky, noticing that Josh was still only in midfield, wasn't pleased. 'Stop whinging, Foggy! Just get on with the game,' the coach called sharply. Ricky knew he wasn't being fair but there were times when Foggy irritated him. And this was one of those times. He saw Karen Rowley was watching him so he swung away and hurried over to the bench.

'A word with you, Davey,' he murmured, continuing his walk so they'd be out of earshot of Jane. Davey's blue eyes brightened at the sudden prospect of getting on to the pitch. 'So, how d'you rate our chances this season, Davey. Not your personal chances – the team's.'

'Oh, great, Boss,' was the confident answer. 'Could win the League.'

'Certainly could. *If* everybody plays together, for the team, for the Kings.' He paused and then added, 'Are you sure you're totally committed to the Kings, Davey?'

'Absolutely, Boss. I know I've got competition for the main striker's spot but I'm going to fight for it. To get it for myself, I mean.'

Ricky's eyebrows were ascending. 'Sure about that? You haven't felt you might be better off with another team? One where you can see a regular place for yourself? After all, a lot of people know you're a prolific goal-scorer in school matches.'

Davey sighed deeply, his smile fading. 'OK, Boss, I get it. You know I've had a trial with Redville, don't you?'

'Oh, I *do* know that, Davey. Nothing much escapes me about what goes on in our Sunday League. It's part of my job to keep my finger on the pulse. If somebody I'd like in my team becomes available I want to know about it. Equally, if one of my squad is thinking of a move I want to know about that, too. Very much want to know about it. An unhappy player can do a lot of damage among his squad-mates.'

'Boss, it wasn't like that,' Davey insisted. He wondered why Ricky felt the need to go through all that rigmarole, all those questions, turning his trial into a kind of soap opera. Why hadn't he simply asked outright why Davey had been tested by Redville. Quite plainly, Ricky knew the whole story, or enough of it to query his loyalty.

'So what was it like?' Ricky kept on. 'Tell me, because I don't know what it is that appeals to you about playing for someone else.'

Davey decided that honesty was the best course of action. If he tried to make anything up the Boss would be sure to recognize the invention. 'Well, you know I didn't get many first-team chances last season, Alex was in great form and then we had Karl-Heinz playing for us and Josh was up front most of the time. I mean, he's a striker today, isn't he? That's the job he always wants. He loves scoring goals for the Kings. We *all* do, Boss.'

Ricky wasn't really listening. His attention had switched back to the match because Kellington were attacking again, attacking in strength this time. Josh, stranded in midfield, had been bypassed and the greyhound-fast winger was cutting through the centre. Without warning he suddenly lifted the ball towards the far post where another attacker darted across in front of Kieren Kelly. Kieren was slow to see the danger and before he could react the attacker rose with immaculate timing and powered a downwards header inside the post. Danny leapt but the ball had been directed perfectly.

The goal was greeted with wild rejoicings by the Kellington contingent. Most of those supporters hadn't believed their team was capable of scoring a goal of such classical grace and simplicity. For them, the season couldn't have had a better start. They cheered their players all the way back to their own half.

Ricky's fists were clenching and unclenching. Davey hadn't ever seen him look as fierce as he did at that moment. The Boss could be quite critical on the training ground and all the players expected that, it was what coaches were supposed to be. During a match he usually didn't display much emotion when things went wrong. Davey guessed, and he was absolutely right, that the Boss didn't want the opposition to have the satisfaction of seeing that they'd upset him, that he might be worried about the Kings' performance. He also guessed, again correctly, that when they resumed their conversation Ricky's mood would have darkened.

'Go on, son, you haven't told me anything I don't know about the team,' he snapped.

'Well, I just thought I might stand a better chance of playing with another team,' Davey murmured. 'I mean, you're not likely to drop Alex for very long, are you? So that means there's only one place up front that's up for grabs. And, well, Josh is playing striker again today. I'm on the bench and I HATE it!'

For a few minutes the coach didn't say anything but gazed at the pitch as if he were thinking what he should do about this setback for the Kings. Davey wondered whether he'd said the wrong thing, whether the coach would now hate *him* for declaring his feelings so strongly. But he hadn't got anywhere by *not* speaking out so he wasn't really putting his place at risk.

'I'm sorry you think I'd let a family relationship stand in the way of the best interests of the team, Davey,' Ricky said eventually, looking as wounded as he sounded. 'The team comes first with me, *always*. That's why Alex isn't a first choice today. At present, he seems to have lost his touch. When he recovers it we'll think again. I doubt, somehow, whether he'll be selected for the next match against Redville. Yes, nice coincidence that, isn't it?'

Davey blinked. 'Really? So, who'll take his place, Boss? If that happens, I mean. Josh or Foggy?'

'No, you will. It'll be a chance for you to test your real loyalty. So –'

'Ricky, I think Kieren's taken a knock – but the ref hasn't noticed,' Jane Allenby interrupted them. 'Can we do something?'

Belatedly, Ricky switched his attention to the play and saw that Kieren, the slimly built

61

back-line defender, was hobbling around the edge of the box. Plainly he was hurt but it seemed not to have occurred to him to sit down or make for the touch-line where he could receive attention. Ricky frowned. He hadn't seen any incident or tackle in which the boy might have been involved. Obviously, neither had the referee.

'Kieren, what's the trouble, son?' Ricky yelled as he moved sharply along the touch-line to a point near to him. 'Want to come off?'

Kieren shook his head but pain lines were visible on his face. Fortunately for him, the Kings were attacking and so he had time to recover. He didn't want to admit that the injury had occurred when he'd simply turned sharply after attempting a tackle and caught his foot in a divot mark. He was just as concerned about his mother. There were times when she sounded off about soccer becoming increasingly violent and that no one was safe from those 'who tackle like maniacs'. So he was fearful that if he was seen to be hurt she might try to prevent him from playing for the Kings. That, he felt, would destroy him.

'Is everything all right?' Jane enquired as Ricky turned back towards her. She thought he looked as if he were in another world. He seemed to have lost interest in the game.

'Well, he says so,' he replied. 'What happened?'

'Didn't see it myself,' Jane had to admit. 'I don't think he's imagining it, though. Kieren's too keen for that. Ricky, are you thinking of making any tactical changes? I mean our forwards are just not combining, are they? It's not surprising with Josh staying back most of the time.'

'We'll give it another minute or two to see what happens,' Ricky replied, looking at his watch. 'Half-time is five minutes away. I'll sort things out then.'

By then, however, the Kings were two goals down and in deep trouble, trouble of their own making. For when Kellington sprang another attack, this time down the central channel, Joe Parbold contrived to put the ball in his own net. It was the speed of the attack that caught them all out. Once again the prime mover was the electric winger, chipping the ball cleverly across the box and yelling for a return. The Kings' defence was stretched and when Joe lunged at the winger to intercept the ball he succeeded only in diverting it wide of Danny Loxham. The ball hadn't much pace on it after that but enough to send it trickling into the net just inside the post.

'Unbelievable!' exclaimed Jane Allenby while some of the parents' comments would not have been printable.

Ricky didn't say a word but the moment the whistle sounded for the interval he strode towards the dressing-room, lightning flashing in his eyes.

4 *Walk Out*

Joe was slumped on the bench, head down, speaking to no one, when Ricky walked in. All too plainly, the Rock had crumbled. 'Boss, I didn't do it on purpose, honest. Couldn't get to the ball properly.'

'I know, Joe, I know,' replied Ricky, his attitude softening a little as he took in Joe's ashen features. 'I don't want to blame you personally for the scoreline. We're *all* responsible for that. We're all to blame.'

His son shot him a quick glance but didn't say anything. Alex had been bouncing a ball against the far wall but he abandoned that the moment his father came in because he knew it irritated him. All the same, he didn't want to be branded as one of the culprits: he hadn't been given a chance to show what he could do against Kellington. Maybe, though, his dad was intending to make changes immediately. Surely there was no point in persevering with a partnership up front that had proved a complete failure?

For once, Ricky wasn't certain what he should be telling his players, though he was anxious to prevent them from recognizing that fact. In all the time he'd been in charge, which amounted to more than an entire season, he couldn't remember an occasion when they'd so ignored his instructions about the way they were to play. If he started to criticize individuals then he'd have to go through the whole team.

'Listen, Boss, I know I should've been playing as a striker but, well, I knew the defence needed me, so I had to help out,' Josh suddenly confessed.

'No, we didn't, we could manage fine on our own,' muttered Kieren Kelly. 'We were doing OK until you came back and *disorganized* us. So –'

'Rubbish!' Josh retaliated. 'You needed me. My headers got us out of trouble, remember?'

'The big trouble is I'm out on my own up front,' Foggy claimed. 'I've just got to have support. I can't do everything on my own.'

'Really?' Danny cut in with a laugh. 'I've always heard you say you can do *everything* by yourself. You're a sort of one-man fire brigade!'

That caused a few smiles and a lessening of tension. Lloyd, in particular, enjoyed that comment but he wasn't going to say anything in case it wasn't to Ricky Todd's liking. It seemed to Lloyd this would be the worst time to irritate him.

'If I was the captain, which I should be, then I would sort everything out in no time,' Foggy hit back. 'Craziest thing in the world to have a captain who's a *goalie*!'

'Foggy, we're not going through all that again,' Ricky said. 'I let you all have a chance to say something positive in the hope you'd recognize where the trouble stems from. Instead, all you do is bicker. That's helping nobody. If we go on like this the second half will be a massacre. Yes, a massacre. And we'll be the ones lying dead at the end of it.'

Alex decided this was the moment to speak. He'd been mulling it over for much of his time on the bench so he'd worked out what he hoped would be effective phrases.

'Listen, we've got to have somebody up front who knows what he's doing, who *wants* to play there. And that's me. I'm a *real* centre-forward, a *real* striker. Josh isn't any good there. So put me on and put Josh somewhere else.'

Almost in unison, the rest of the players turned to look at Ricky to see what he'd do now. Alex had always been outspoken and they were all aware how arrogant he could be, but they'd never supposed he would speak to his father like this, however upset he was.

'Alex, I'm not getting into a discussion about how *you* feel about your role in the team. I've got a team to think about, not just one player's moanings.' He spoke quite mildly but didn't actually look at his son. He just wished Alex would shut up or disappear.

Alex, fiercely brushing his eyebrows, suddenly jumped to his feet, shaking his hair back. 'OK, that's it,' he announced. 'I'm off. And you can forget about me for the future as well. I'll find a team that *does* want me.'

Without a backward glance he strode out of the dressing-room. Somehow it was the fact that he opened and then closed the door quietly that impressed his team-mates more than anything else. All too obviously, he wasn't bluffing; or, if he was, then this was a different Alex from any they'd seen previously. Once again, every eye swivelled towards the coach. How on earth would he deal with such a rebellion?

Ricky's first thought was to send somebody, Danny perhaps, to call Alex back but then he realized how unfair that would be on Danny if Alex failed to respond. Knowing Alex's capacity to sulk on occasions, he guessed the defiance would continue and so Danny wouldn't be able to persuade him to return. So he did nothing, a moment of weakness he would regret.

His second mistake was to tell Foggy that the would-be skipper was right, he did need help up front and that it would be provided in the second half. Foggy, of course, would make a lot of mileage out of that in the weeks ahead but for the present he simply smirked and waited to see what was intended. Davey, as astonished as anyone by Alex's outburst, listened with eager anticipation. Surely he'd get his chance now?

'Josh, I know you've been a tower of strength in defence but for the rest of this match I want you to put everything you know into *attacking* Kellington, attacking non-stop, not giving their defence a split-second's peace. We've got to pressure them. You and Marc have got to be twin battering-rams, OK? Batter down the front door of their fortress.'

It was a phrase that had just occurred to him and he liked the sound of it. So, apparently, did Josh. He was so thankful he'd not been blamed for the present scoreline and banished altogether. Josh was as desperate as ever to win matches for the Kings and he made a vow he wouldn't play out of his position again whatever the state of the game.

'Boss, I'll fling myself at them as if I were wearing the best body-armour in the world!' Josh declared. He sounded so serious that most of the boys laughed. At last, the depression in the dressing-room lifted a little.

When they went out for the second half without any other discussions about tactical changes having taken place nearly everyone looked first towards the bench to see whether

Alex had changed his mind. But there was no sign of him.

'Did you see Alex come out?' Ricky felt obliged to ask Jane who had just broken away from talking to Kieren's mother, Jakki.

'No. Why, what's happened?'

Ricky told her as briefly as possible and was thankful it didn't occur to Jane to enquire whether he felt Alex should be disciplined. That was something he didn't want to think about yet, though he knew that for the sake of team morale the matter couldn't be ignored.

'I'm sure Alex will come round when he's had time to think it over,' Jane suggested with the aim of comforting him. Ricky, however, suspected Alex would do nothing of the sort. His sulks could last a long time and threats of punishment often went unheeded.

'Well, it's to be hoped we don't get any injuries now we're down to just one sub,' she went on. 'Still, I'm sure Davey is pleased to have the chance of getting a game.'

Because she had a good carrying voice Davey heard that and his hopes immediately rose. Dominic's mum was someone he liked and he was sure he'd do a lot better with the Kings if only she were the coach. He couldn't imagine that happening: Ricky Todd had gone to a lot of trouble to get the coach's job from Sam Saxton so he wasn't likely to give it up in a hurry.

'Come on, Ricky, get 'em going. We can't be starting the season with a defeat,' one of the supporters sang out; and those spectators around him murmured their agreement. 'This lot look weak at the back so our forwards should be stretching them on the flanks.'

Ricky nodded that he'd heard the comment, not that he agreed with it. Since becoming coach he'd realized just how many spectators thought they knew how to do his job better than he did. Everyone seemed to be an expert these days, especially on the subject of schoolboy soccer. He'd forgotten that he'd been exactly the same when Sam was in charge.

Kellington weren't going to give their opponents much chance to exploit that alleged weakness in defence. They resumed on the attack, their electric winger rapidly switching flanks before again cutting inside and then delivering a precision cross to his co-attacker. But he could do nothing because, timing his sliding tackle perfectly, Joe took the ball from his toes and then, getting to his feet, nudged the ball away for Kieren to complete the clearance. Kieren had now run off the discomfort in his ankle and was thankful Ricky had not noticed his limp earlier.

Ricky uttered a sigh of relief: the Rock had demonstrated he'd got over his trauma in the first half and was back in reliable form. Some neat interchanges in midfield resulted in the ball being whipped out to Lloyd on the wing.

'That's more like it!' yelled the Kings' most vocal supporter. But he spoke too soon for Lloyd failed to control the ball on a bumpy stretch and was easily dispossessed. Ricky grimaced but didn't say anything. There was nothing to be gained by chastising anyone at present. They knew what was expected of them so they had to work out their own salvation on the pitch. The coach became aware though that Lloyd's mum was continuously casting glances in his direction as if to see whether the coach had noticed *her*. As she was wearing one of her colourful skirts – this time the purple almost matched the team's shirts – it would have been impossible to miss her. The next time she caught his eye Ricky raised his eyebrows and nodded a greeting, but Serena just frowned and looked away again.

'Lloyd seems a bit out of sorts today,' Jane remarked to him in little more than a whisper. 'D'you think it might be time to replace him with Davey?'

'Definitely not! Much too soon for that. We're down to one sub as it is so we've got to hold him back in case of an emergency, a serious injury or something.' Ricky paused and then added forlornly, 'I mean, doesn't look as if Alex's coming back, does it?'

Jane made no response; it hadn't occurred to her that Alex might be permitted to resume his sub's role after deserting the team at half-time. It was up to Ricky how he handled that sort of behaviour but for the good of the rest of the Kings he shouldn't be allowed to get away with it.

Moments later, as if to underline the coach's caution, Foggy Thrale went down under a strong challenge. Normally he'd get up and let his anger blaze away at the culprit but this time he stayed down, writhing in real or vividly imagined agony. Jane dashed on to the pitch even before the ref summoned her.

Foggy didn't even move when she knelt beside him. When she managed to get him to roll over on to his back she was astonished to see tears in the eyes of the boy who prided himself on his toughness as well as his foghorn voice. He was clutching his knee and Jane could see the red mark caused by an opponent's boot.

'Marc, how bad is it?' she enquired as, gently but firmly, her fingers pressed the injury zone. 'D'you think you can stand?'

He shook his head and the ref, standing over them, plainly anxious to get on with the match, said at once, 'You'll have to go off, son. Can't hold up play any longer for a little knock. Better get some help, missus.'

Jane hated being talked to like that but this wasn't the moment to lodge objections. Lloyd and Dominic were the nearest two Kings and she asked them to carry Marc to the touch-line in a fireman's lift. Dominic didn't seem keen but he couldn't refuse. Jane, following with her medical bag, was still actually on the pitch when the game restarted. In spite of her concern for the injury she registered the fact that the ref hadn't even spoken to the offender let alone cautioned him. She'd never been anti-referees as some coaches and fans were but she was sure this official wasn't really up to his job.

'How's it feel now, Foggy?' she enquired as Dominic and Lloyd raced back to the action and Ricky wandered over to see the extent of the problem.

The coach asked; 'Any chance you can carry on?'

To Jane's surprise, Foggy sat up and, brushing his hand across his eyes, said, 'Think so, Boss. I mean, it is a *bit* better.' Doubtless that was because Jane had applied the painkilling spray, though she wouldn't expect it to be quite so effective so soon. Was this a case of a boy who felt he could win sympathy from her but not from the man who controlled his football? She'd had very little to do with Marc Thrale since becoming assistant coach, though no one could overlook his boisterous personality. She felt she was learning.

'Good, then I want you back in the front line, going hammer and tongs at 'em,' Ricky told him. 'Let's signal the ref.'

It was as Foggy was trotting back on to the pitch that the coach turned to the boy who'd come to stand beside them. 'Not the moment to put you on yet, son,' he said cheerfully. 'Plenty of time left.' And so Davey, looking just as dejected as he felt, returned to the bench. Jane gave him a sympathetic smile but Davey couldn't respond.

'That was a diabolical tackle, you know,' Jane pointed out to Ricky. 'But he didn't so much as wave a finger at the culprit, did he, that hopeless ref.'

'Don't know, didn't see the incident – was looking somewhere else at the time,' Ricky confessed.

Jane was astonished. How could a coach have missed something as obvious as that? Was he losing interest in the game altogether? The Ricky Todd she could see now seemed totally different from the passionate enthusiast she was used to; and he was light years away from the man who only the previous year had rushed on to the pitch, ready to assault a ref until his own son, Alex, managed to stop him. That was before Ricky became the Kings' coach. Many people remarked at the time and later that although the action was completely wrong at least he proved how much he cared about the game and the injustice shown to his son. That passion was no longer in evidence these days, Jane decided. Instead, Ricky simply looked abstracted as if his mind were on something worlds away from football.

On the pitch Kellington were cutting deep into the Kings' defence again and a quick exchange of passes on the edge of the penalty area provided them with a clear shooting chance after their main striker had easily turned Kieren. Matthew Forrest should have been more watchful in the first place so he, like the rest of the defence, looked relieved when Danny brought off a flying save and turned the ball round a post.

'Come on, Kings, get a grip – mark your men – don't let them get another goal,' Jane yelled at them as they took up positions for the corner kick. She hadn't intended to shout as loudly as that – she hadn't intended to shout at all – but it seemed to her that *somebody* in authority should be saying something positive. She glanced at Ricky in case he disapproved but he showed no reaction at all. What was he thinking of? she couldn't help wondering.

The corner came to naught, fortunately, and Jane, eager to display her support, now called, 'Come on, Kings, let's attack, attack, attack. Remember, Kings rule!'

That was the team's rallying cry invented, she believed, by Ricky himself, and it often seemed to stir the side to greater effort. It did now as Tree, recovering his composure, hit a long and accurate pass to Foggy. Suddenly, Foggy's limp disappeared as he sensed the chance of a goal. Of course, he couldn't beat every opponent, willing though he was to try, and so he parted with the ball on the edge of the box for Lloyd to continue the movement. Lloyd, having received little support so far from anyone, decided this was the moment for glory. After tricking the Kellington back-four player watching him, Lloyd looked up, saw the goalkeeper off his line and tried to lob him.

The intention was good but the execution weak, one spectator saying loud enough for everyone to hear that it was 'pitiful'. The ball flew up but far too high to have any chance of falling under the crossbar; to make things worse, Lloyd even managed to impart some spin so that it curved away from the goal-mouth altogether. Lloyd's shoulders drooped as he turned round to trudge back for the goal-kick.

'Come on, Lloyd, you can do better than that, son,' Ricky called. 'You didn't need to shoot from that distance. Go further in next time.' Then he turned to Jane and murmured, 'Got plenty of talent, that boy, but just doesn't seem able to make it work for him.'

'Pity he didn't score just then,' Jane replied diplomatically. 'I expect a goal would do wonders for his confidence.'

It would have done a lot for the confidence of anyone playing for or supporting the Kings but a goal didn't arrive until it was too late to affect the state of the game. When Foggy crumpled up after another careless tackle and

Jane rushed on to attend to the stricken striker, Ricky decided the time had come to make the only change that was open to him. After a quick survey of those present at the match revealed that Alex hadn't returned he told Davey Stroud to prepare for action.

Davey's eyes lit up immediately and he had his track-suit top off before the coach completed his instructions. 'Just go for everything, Davey, really put yourself about, make 'em know you're there. You've got the energy the rest of them seem to be lacking. Maybe we haven't trained hard enough pre-season. Half the team are looking exhausted already.'

'Will Josh be dropping back then, Boss?' Davey wanted to know. 'I mean, am I supposed to be linking with Foggy.'

'Foggy's coming off and Josh is staying in attack, though he hasn't contributed much yet,' was the reply. 'You just do your best for us, son, and for yourself. I've got lots of faith in you, Davey.'

Davey didn't believe that but it didn't matter. He was on the pitch and he was going to score, he was absolutely convinced of that.

It was how he felt about every match he played. At school he'd been told by a visiting professional player that he possessed the instinct of a real striker, 'someone who just knows how to be in the right place at the right time'. He had never forgotten those words. What annoyed him was that too many coaches seemed not to agree with him. All they cared about was his height or, as they regarded it, his lack of it.

The towering Josh ought to have been Davey's perfect partner and within a minute of his coming on to the pitch the relationship appeared to have been forged in heaven. Deep into the Kellington half, Reuben Jones took a free kick for a minor infringement and swung the ball to the far side of the penalty area. With splendid timing Josh rose above everyone and headed the ball down to Davey. In spite of an awkward bounce the ball came under Davey's instant control and, darting past his marker, he flicked it sideways and into Josh's path. Josh thumped it with a full swing of his right leg and the ball simply flew like a cannon shot into the roof of the net almost before the goalie could move a muscle.

'At last!' Ricky yelled and most supporters echoed that before hastily looking at watches to see whether there was still time for an equalizer. Two minutes at most was the opinion of the majority.

'Nice timing, that substitution,' Jane smiled at Ricky. Personally she felt he ought to have put Davey on sooner but there was no point in saying so.

Ricky just nodded, glad that it had worked. A goal like that might shake Kellington to their foundations and so maybe they'd concede another. The coach hated the idea of losing the opening match of the season.

That chance came without warning – and vanished just as quickly. Just as Ricky had supposed, Kellington panicked when the Kings threatened again. A defender thought that safety first meant passing back to his keeper when caught in possession on the edge of the box. Lloyd, who'd come infield to support the strikers, darted forward, stuck out a leg and managed to divert the ball across the face of the goal. Davey, already on the move and anticipating Lloyd's man-oeuvre, pounced, swung his right foot – and missed the ball completely. Before Davey could recover his balance after that horrendous stumble, the Kellington goalie swooped, scooped up the ball in both arms and then took his time in clearing it upfield. Seconds later the whistle went for full-time and Kellington celebrated like a team that's just won a major trophy rather than an ordinary League game.

The coaches shook hands with predictably mixed emotions. Kellington's was inclined to be generous. 'Think we were a bit lucky today – didn't see how your boy could miss that sitter in front of goal. Still, our sponsor swore that green and white would be lucky colours for us. Seems he's right! Best of luck to you for the rest of the season – until you play us again, anyway!'

None of the Kings was as devastated as Davey. 'Boss, I can't believe it,' he came over to tell Ricky. 'I mean, I've never done anything as bad as that before. I'm not making excuses but the ball must have bobbled on a divot or something.'

'Davey, it's not going to ruin your life. Just try to forget it,' Ricky told him quite gently.

'Every player misses a kick sometimes, bound to.'

'But – but –'

'Davey, I said forget it! The match is over, it's history. You set up a goal, so remember that. If we need to analyse things we'll do it when we've had time to think things over.'

Jane put her arms round Davey's shoulders and gave him a hug. 'Davey, you were hardly on the pitch five minutes, yet you set up Josh's goal and got us back into the game. So, as the Boss says, don't worry. There'll be plenty of other chances coming your way, I'm sure.'

Ricky, listening, didn't say anything more on that subject but he did have a comment about Reuben as he and Jane walked to the dressing-rooms. 'Bit disappointed with our new player's contribution. Hardly seemed to get into the match. I think that's a major reason why we weren't firing on all cylinders. You sure he's the right player for us, that he's going to fit in?'

Jane couldn't help feeling that this implied criticism was really directed at her because she was the one who'd recommended him.

She, too, was disappointed with Reuben's overall performance but he had to be given time to get to know his new team-mates. Moreover, it was his pinpoint cross that had led directly to the Kings' only goal of the game. No doubt Reuben would build on that success if Ricky persevered with him as a playmaker. She said most of that to Ricky but he just grunted as if he agreed with her but wasn't prepared to say so at present.

'Are you all right, Ricky?' she enquired. 'I mean, you don't seem your usual self. And I suspect that's not just due to the match result, is it?'

He paused and gave her a wan smile. 'Very perceptive of you, Jane. Physically I'm OK but I do have a lot on my mind at present. This defeat by a team we should have walloped doesn't help, I admit. But we'll get over it, won't we? We have to. Anyway, I hope I can sort everything out on Tuesday evening. I'll be in touch before then, though. See if we can come up with some fresh ideas for the next match. Must win that one.'

Jane nodded vigorously. 'Definitely. Can't have the Kings losing their crown. So give me a call when you've got a moment. Oh, and I hope everything works out with Alex. I'm sure he's just going through one of those rebellious phases that seem to affect most boys of his age.'

She wasn't sure how much of that he'd heard because he'd already swung round and, head down, was reaching for the dressing-room door.

5 *Phone In*

Jane Allenby hadn't been expecting a call
from Jakki Kelly but she was always pleased
to chat with any of the other mums of the
Kings' players. Normally they were all united
in supporting the team and most were
prepared to do all manner of chores to help
out when necessary, though few were as
hard-working as Karen Rowley who
personally laundered the players' kit after
every match.

'So what did you think of yesterday's
performance?' enquired Jakki. As if certain
that there couldn't be any alternative view
she immediately offered her own, 'Pretty
dire, wasn't it?'

'Well, I wouldn't go as far as that, Jakki,'
Jane responded cautiously. 'The defence was
a bit mixed up at times and they didn't seem
to know whether Josh was one of them or

what. I mean, he was chosen as a striker but kept dropping back. Still, I'm sure things will be sorted out for the next match and Ricky –'

'Kieren's worried, you know,' Jakki interrupted. 'He says he's never sure whether Ricky really rates him. If he isn't playing in a settled back-four all the time, well, he's no chance of catching the selectors' eye, has he? Kieren's always looking towards his long-term future, you know.'

Jane didn't know that. She considered Kieren a perfectly competent defender but hadn't seen him as a future star. On the other hand, the Kings were at an age when talent might blossom overnight; or seem to disappear just as quickly. So it was hard to predict how good any player might be a year hence. Still, it was good to know Kieren was ambitious.

'Oh, I'm sure Ricky's got Kieren's interests at heart,' she said soothingly. 'He's always stressing the importance of team effort. That's why he doesn't often sing the praises of individuals in the way another coach might. Don't worry about it, Jakki.'

'I *am* worried,' was the instant retort. 'I'm

very worried about the direction the team's taking. If the Kings are going to get to the top, to win Cups, to fulfil all that promise they've got, well, we can't afford another defeat like yesterday's. We've got to do something about it.'

'Jakki, it was only the first match of the season. There's months to go yet. Things'll get better, I know they will.' She realized she was repeating almost the exact words she used to patients who were inclined to panic at the onset of a pain or severe discomfort: they were convinced they'd die or suffer some appalling tragedy. 'So let's –'

'Jane, it's easy to say it's only one game,' Mrs Kelly cut in again. 'But if the signs of trouble are so obvious, things will get worse rather than better. So it's best to act as fast as possible. I mean, a relegation season is more likely to begin with a defeat than a win, isn't it? That's what Kieren says and I'm inclined to agree with him. Kieren's very good on statistics. He studies the history of football as if he needed it for university entrance.'

The Kings' assistant coach hesitated before

asking, 'So what d'you think ought to be done? Obviously you've been discussing matters in some depth, you and Kieren – and Clark?'

Jakki ignored that reference to her husband and went off on another tack altogether. 'Do you think Ricky's got problems? I mean, he looked pretty desperate at times yesterday. Either that or his mind wasn't on football at all. I've been wondering if everything's all right at home because, plainly, there's been some trouble with Alex.'

Jane had no intention of getting into that kind of gossip. In a village like Rodale Kings rumours of any kind spread like a bush fire and the innocent could be consumed rapidly. 'I've really no idea about that, Jakki. I can tell you that Ricky hasn't confided anything to me. All I do know is that he wants the best for the Kings, as we all do. Look, I'll have to go. I got home only two minutes before you rang and my last patient was *very* demanding!'

'Jane, I'm glad we've had this chat. Do remember what I said: it's better to take action soon instead of waiting for an emergency. Go and put your feet up. I'll talk to you again soon.'

That same evening Ricky, too, had just got in from work at his furniture factory when the phone rang and he was the only one around to answer it because Melanie, his wife, was away visiting her mother. He assumed it was another business call because there'd been a stream of those lately. However, it turned out to be Taylor Hill, owner of a bistro in the High Street and father of Lawrence, a midfielder on the fringe of the Kings' squad. Like many a midfielder Lawrence, or Larry as he preferred, wanted to be a striker.

After the usual opening pleasantries Mr Hill remarked, 'I expect you're deep in thought about our team, aren't you, Ricky?'

'Well, I've actually got rather more important matters on my mind at present,' the coach replied rather unwisely.

He could sense the surprise at the other end of the line. Then, as if testing the water, his caller said lightly, 'Can there be anything more important than the Kings?'

'Yes, my company comes first. You know,

the way I earn my living. Without that nothing else is possible, is it?'

'Oh, so the rumours are true, then, are they? I wasn't ringing about that but, well, as you've mentioned it . . .'

'Rumours? What rumours?' Ricky asked sharply.

'You can't keep secrets in a place as small as Rodale Kings, Ricky, you ought to know that. The word going round is that you're selling up, getting out of the furniture trade. None of my business, really, but . . .'

'No, I'm not getting out in the way you mean, Taylor. But there has been a takeover bid. From a Scandinavian company, in fact. I'm trying to negotiate the best terms possible for my staff and workforce. That's what's going on. But things are a long way from being settled. So if rumours swirl round you again you'll be able to put the record straight, won't you?'

Taylor Hill either didn't sense the sarcasm or chose to ignore it. 'Well, thanks for putting me in the picture, Ricky. Just hope everything works out for you personally. Don't want to think of Rodale Kings without you. Now, what I really rang about was the game against Kellington. Bit of a set-back, that, wasn't it? To put it *mildly*. I mean, are we going to improve for the next game?'

'I've got plenty of good players so I'll be able to sort things out, I expect. Now –'

'Ah, but will your Alex be one of them, Ricky? I think that's pretty relevant to our future, don't you?' Taylor Hill said smoothly.

'Don't think I understand the point you're making,' replied Ricky, though he was sure he understood it all too well. He simply wanted to know the extent of his caller's criticisms.

'Well, I'm sorry to say it, Ricky, but it was plain to a lot of us who support the team that Alex was sulking, we've seen him do it before when things haven't gone in his favour. I'm full of admiration for the way in which you sent him away. Good discipline, that. But that sort of thing's bound to affect team morale, isn't it?'

Ricky hadn't expected it to be as strong as this but there was no point in trying to deny what had happened: once more, rumour had done its work well. He guessed that Mr Hill was simply being generous in suggesting Ricky had dismissed Alex rather than that Alex had walked out. As a keen supporter, the man was entitled to his opinion, just as he was entitled to ask about future plans. It was just unfortunate he was ringing about it now, late into an evening, instead of raising the matter at the weekly training session which all parents and supporters were welcome to attend.

'Look, Taylor, I think Alex is my problem. I'm the one he's mad at so I'll deal with it. And *firmly*, I can promise. Sulking, as you put it, is childish, petty. I'm not tolerating it. Don't worry, though, there are plenty of good players in the squad, all keen to win things with the Kings. We're not going to collapse because of one shock defeat. Now –'

'Oh, does that mean you'll be looking for new talent up front? I mean, after the way young Davey Stroud missed that complete sitter you've got to have someone who knows how to put the ball in the net.' His pause was fractional before he added, 'Like my Lawrence, for instance. At school and everywhere he's scoring goals like a running tap you can't turn off.'

Ricky was annoyed with himself for not seeing the real purpose behind Taylor Hill's phone call. While it was true that Larry could always be relied upon to turn up for training and play his heart out in practice games he had never shown exceptional talent; he wasn't particularly tall or strong and it had never occurred to the coach that Larry Hill might become an instinctive, lethal striker. Fathers were inclined to overrate the abilities of sons (and he wasn't excluding himself from that category). Taylor was no different from the rest, he merely wanted the best for his boy. Ricky decided his best move would be to play it cool, to overlook Taylor's rather cynical way of trying to cash in on Alex's present disaffection with the Kings.

'Must say, I hadn't heard about Larry's successes as a striker,' he replied pleasantly. 'So let's see if he can do it for the Kings. I'll put him through his paces on Tuesday evening. OK?'

'Excellent, Ricky, excellent! I'm sure you won't be disappointed. Now, another thing –'

'Sorry, Taylor got to go. That's my mobile ringing now. Probably about the company. Cheers. See you Tuesday.'

While he was speaking to Dominic Allenby, Danny had the phone cradled under his chin because he needed both hands to unwrap a stick of chewing-gum, a recently acquired habit.

'Well, you're the captain,' Dominic was saying, 'so you should know more than the rest of us. I mean, doesn't Ricky Todd tell you what's going on?'

'No, never. He just does what he wants. So I go along with it. I mean, what else can I do?'

'But you said you were going to talk to Alex, see what's happening to him. If we don't score goals we're never going to win games. And I fancied us for the title this season.'

'I did try to talk to Alex but he didn't want to know,' Danny revealed. 'When I rang I got Ricky but he said he was too busy to talk to me. So I asked about Alex. Well, the Boss said he was fed up with all that nonsense from

Alex, you know, complaining about being ignored. Honest, that's how he said it, Dom. He said that if Alex didn't apologize for walking out, for his *stupidity*, there's no way he'll play for the Kings again under his managership. He seemed really mad, Dom. That's why I couldn't ask anything else.'

'So you never got to talk to Alex?'

'Oh yes I did. Ricky handed the phone over to him. But Alex said he didn't want to talk, either. Said he was totally turned off the Kings. They didn't want him and he didn't want them, us, I mean. Says he has other plans and another team's interested in him. But that's all I could get out of him.'

'*If* he's got other plans.'

'Oh, I think he has. That other team really could be after him. He's not going to give up soccer. Point is, you can't win against your dad, can you? He's always going to have the last word.'

'Same thing with mums, too,' Dominic said softly but feelingly.

'Wouldn't know about that, would I? Never see my mum. But your mum is easy to get on with, Dom. Does a good job for us, doesn't she? In fact, she seems to know loads about soccer now. I think she'd be a good replacement if ever Ricky decided to pack the game in. And he just might if Alex stays away.'

'Oh, don't say that, Danny! About Mum, I mean. It'd make things bad for me. She's already talking football non-stop at home. I'd never have my own space if Mum took over the Kings. I'd be under a permanent microscope!'

'Maybe,' Danny agreed. 'But it might be good for us if we have a coach who can see us clearly and knows how to get the best out of us. Ricky Todd's no longer like that.'

Because he was immersed in his favourite TV soap Foggy was reluctant to take the call when Alex rang and his mother had to tell him twice that he was wanted.

'Yeah, what is it?' he bellowed into the receiver.

Alex would've had to hold the phone away from his ear even if Foggy had spoken in his normal tone. Now he felt deafened but staged a quick recovery. This could be a very important conversation. 'Foggy, are you happy playing for the Kings?'

'What's that supposed to mean?' was the unhelpful reply.

'Look, Fogs, you know you want to be a striker and Dad won't let you – well, not usually. He doesn't pick me, either. So I've decided to pack it in with the Kings and find another team. Maybe even start a new one. So how about you doing the same? I mean, you're going nowhere with the Kings, are you?'

Foggy's suspicions were aroused. 'Has your dad put you up to this? Is this his way of trying to get rid of me?'

Alex was tempted to agree because that, he realized, would work to his advantage. But he couldn't take the risk because Foggy was perfectly capable of contacting Ricky direct and challenging him to deny such charges. 'No way!' was the calculated reply. 'My dad knows nothing about this. We're not even talking at present. I've told you, I'm getting out before it's too late.'

'Too late for what?' Foggy was smart enough to ask.

'Too late for us to get into another team before the season's half over. You know, you can't get your registration cancelled after more than five matches. Well, I think it's five. And, anyway, other teams will have got most of the players they want.'

'Any team'd want me!' Foggy retorted with a burst of his usual self-confidence. 'So –'

'Exactly! And they'd want me, too, Fogs. If we offered a top team the pair of us in one go they'd snap our hands off to sign us up. We're – er – irresistible! How about it?'

Foggy could hear raised voices from the TV set. Tonight's episode was obviously reaching a climax. He couldn't miss that. 'Alex, I'll think about it. Go to go now. Cheers, mate.'

At the other end of the line Alex muttered a curse, gritted his teeth and looked at his list for the next numbers to punch in.

Because the noise of the water was so loud Davey didn't even hear the bathroom door opening let alone the sound of the phone ringing. So it was a surprise when his dad tweaked aside the shower curtain and announced, 'You're wanted! Urgently, apparently.'

'What?' enquired Davey, whose mind had been full of football images and sequences, most of them featuring himself.

'Davey, get the water out of your ears fast. You're wanted on the phone so you'll need to listen properly. Turn the water off and come out now.'

Reluctantly, Davey did as he was told and accepted the towel his father was holding out. 'Hey, I was enjoying that,' he complained. 'Couldn't I just ring back later? Who is it? Kieren, I'll bet. Or –'

'No, it's not one of your mates. It's somebody called Kingston. Said something about a red bill or a –'

'Greg Kingston? He's the coach of *Redville*! But what does he want?'

'You'll never find out if you don't answer the phone. He won't hang on for ever. Go on, hurry up, and try not to drip water *everywhere*.'

Holding the towel in place Davey shot downstairs, wishing for the umpteenth time that his mum and dad weren't so implacably opposed to mobile phones. Already he was working out what Mr Kingston must want of him and how he should respond. Why on earth couldn't he have phoned a week ago instead of now?

'Sorry to be so long, Mr Kingston,' he apologized instantly. 'I was in the shower.'

'I don't mind waiting, son, especially in a good cause,' was the smooth response. 'But I must keep this short because I've other calls to make tonight. Depending on you, perhaps. Remember I said I didn't have a place for you in my squad? Well, things've changed. Often do in football. So now there is a vacancy. Point is, Davey, would you like to try your luck with us, sign on for Redville for the season?'

'Mr Kingston, I'd love to but, well, I can't. You see, I'm still with the Goal Kings. I'm registered.'

'Well, might be able to do something about that if you haven't played so far this season. Sometimes the Highlea League rules can be a bit flexible. Depends on the circumstances. Transfers have been known even well into the season for special reasons.'

'But I played in the first match, the one we

lost. I started on the bench but got on for the last few minutes,' Davey explained, wishing now that things had been completely different. He was still having nightmares about missing that open goal. And he still didn't know whether Ricky Todd would keep his promise to play him in the next match.

'Pity about that,' remarked Greg Kingston, though he was thinking only about his own missed chance of signing up a boy who showed much promise and quite probably would develop well with proper coaching, his own brand of coaching, of course. 'Funny thing is, we play your lot next. So it would've been a chance for you to show 'em what they've been missing by not playing you regularly.'

'Yeah, that's right,' Davey had to agree.

'OK, son, we'll have to leave things as they are for now. But coaches always have to look ahead and who knows what might happen by the time *next* season comes around. All the best, then.'

'Thanks, Mr Kingston,' Davey said politely. He was about to replace the receiver when his caller had a final word.

'Oh yes, Davey, just a thought. Don't go taking your revenge on us by scoring against us on Sunday! I wouldn't take kindly to that, you know.'

Davey wasn't sure whether that was a joke or not but, on balance, he thought not. His original impression that the Redville coach didn't possess much of a sense of humour hadn't been changed by this conversation.

Although his sister had shot him a few curious glances while he was on the phone she and his mum were still absorbed by a TV soap and so he didn't have to say anything about his call before he made his way back to the bathroom. By now he was ready for some warm water but this time he decided on a bath rather than a shower.

A few moments later as he lay full-length and soaked up the heat he thought about the conversation with Greg Kingston. Should he have said that he'd be glad of a chance to play for Redville and thus allow the coach to try and arrange a transfer? After all, he had no guarantees that there was a future for him in the Goal Kings' squad. If Alex Todd decided to return to their ranks the probability was that his father would forgive him his rebellion and reinstate him as first choice striker. And that would leave Davey Stroud with little chance of winning a regular slot in the team.

Still, there was one chink of light in the present gloom: Sunday's match against Redville Rangers. Ricky Todd usually kept his promises and so Davey was confident he'd be playing even if Alex did return. This would be his opportunity to *prove* to everyone, his team-mates and the opposition, Ricky Todd and Greg Kingston, that he was the *best* striker for his age they'd ever seen. Above all, he must put the ball in the net. Another missed chance would probably be his last for the Goal Kings – and perhaps for anybody else. A goal on Sunday would be the most vital of his life.

'And Davey Stroud must score this time,' he said aloud. And then, louder still, he added, 'And Davey *does* score – a brilliant, breath-taking goal! What a goal! What a player! And the entire crowd is rising to salute Davey Stroud, goal-scorer supreme.'

6 Revenge Match

Ricky Todd was striding the length of the wooden hut that served as one of the changing-rooms at the ground of Redville Rangers JFC. Somebody had already remarked that it looked like a larger-sized and ramshackle garden shed but at least it provided some shelter and privacy for players who were never thrilled about having to change in the open air at the side of the pitch. On this day, with rain bucketing down, it was a real haven.

'So I'm relying on you not to lose this one,' the coach was saying. 'Defeat in our two opening matches would be a disaster. There's no other word will do. Our season would be half over before it's begun. So let's tear into Redville and score some goals from the word go. Go is half of goal, right?'

In a vacant moment recently that phrase

had popped into his head and he'd remembered it. As a slogan it had a lot to recom-mend it, though it could never replace their chanted cry, 'Goal Kings rule!' On the other hand, as they were far from ruling anything at present it might be a good idea to adopt the new phrase, 'Go is half of goal, so go, go, go!'

None of the players was thinking about words at that moment; all that concerned them was the team's performance and their own roles within the team. Foggy, who always wanted things spelled out, had a question.

'Boss, could you tell us, is Alex ever coming back? I mean, well, we miss him.'

Several players recognized the deviousness of that remark but nobody said a word. Only Davey, who had good reason to feel most aggrieved by it, shot him a sharp glance.

'Marc, this is not the time to talk about that,' the coach replied, frowning. 'But if it's going to help the way you play I'll just say that as far as I'm concerned Alex has turned his back on the Goal Kings. Safest to say that he's going one way and we're going another. So – what was that, Lloyd?'

Lloyd, who'd also had a call from Alex, had whispered to Matthew Forrest, 'Probably he's fixing himself up with another team right this minute.' But he hadn't expected Ricky to be aware of that whisper.

'Er, I was just saying that perhaps Alex is, er, wishing he was here now and, well, playing for us and not somebody else,' Lloyd murmured, wishing *he* were somewhere else.

The frown deepened. 'Have you heard anything definite, Lloyd? Have any of you?'

No one was going to admit a thing so all Ricky got was a row of shaking heads and blank expressions. Davey had wondered whether Alex might have made contact with Greg Kingston and signed for them; after all, he hadn't even played as a sub so far this season so no doubt Kingston would be able to persuade the League to allow him to sign Alex. If Alex wasn't talking at home then it would be a major shock for his dad to see him on the pitch wearing the red and white of Rangers (the shirts were scarlet apart from white sleeves and collar and the socks were a design of red, white and black hoops).

'Right, then, let's forget Alex and

concentrate on ourselves,' Ricky resumed briskly. 'We're the ones who've got to win this match. We've already gone over time and again in training the things we should be doing so I hope nobody's memory is at fault. If it is then changes will be made, you can be certain of that. Any questions?'

He glanced, automatically it seemed, at Foggy, nowadays the most outspoken member of the squad, but Foggy was saying nothing more. The bustling midfielder had been given his chance to make a striker's role his own and he had to make the most of it. Josh was to attack at corners and free kicks around the box but to defend at other times. Foggy wasn't impressed by having Davey as his partner but at least he was unlikely to be outshone by the small, crop-haired attacker. All he envied about Davey was his electric acceleration from almost a standing start. If Foggy possessed that kind of pace then he knew he'd be a world-beater.

'Go on, then, Kings, go out and rule! And do it with style,' Ricky ordered as his players left the hut. 'Give our supporters plenty to cheer about.'

Those spectators were very few in number with rain still falling unrelentingly but they included the Bistro owner, Taylor Hill, whose son Larry was one of the substitutes. Mr Hill had already offered his opinion to everyone who'd listen that Larry was the natural successor to Alex and so should have been on the pitch from the start. Larry, who'd scored a hat-trick for his school earlier in the week, agreed with him.

Jane Allenby was checking her medical bag as Jakki Kelly and Serena Colmer, both under umbrellas, edged down the touch-line towards her. Jane didn't welcome company when she was in her official role as assistant coach and physio but she could hardly ignore mothers of players if they wanted to chat with her. The recent poor weather would have taken some of the sting out of the pitch when players fell and so the boys should finish up with fewer bruises. Doubtless, though, she'd need the sponges and warm water to get rid of mud stains. Mentally she sympathized with Karen Rowley who laundered the players' kit every week. Her washing machine would be working overtime tonight!

'Heard the news?' Jakki greeted her in a loud whisper.

Jane, who'd been hoping for a word with Dominic before the teams lined up, turned with an artificially bright smile. 'Kieren's been picked to play for the County Boys?' she suggested, not meaning a word of it.

'If only . . .' Jakki replied. 'No, about Alex. Did you know he's been trying to start a new team? He's wanting to recruit some of our top players, like Kieren.'

'And Lloyd, too,' Serena put in.

It certainly was news to Jane and her first reaction was to wonder whether Alex had approached Dominic. Her son hadn't said a word about it but probably he wouldn't if he was not interested. And surely Dominic *wouldn't* want to play for anyone but the Kings?

'No, that's news to me,' Jane admitted cheerfully. 'But I can't believe Alex would really desert us. He can sulk, as you know, and I expect he's just going through one of those phases. Happens to most boys, doesn't it?'

'Bit more than a sulk, I hear,' Jakki went

on. 'I gather things are a bit, er, tricky in the Todd household. Ricky's never at home these days. Spending almost every working minute in his furniture factory. Lots of rumours about that, you know.'

'Oh, but that's just the take-over, isn't it?' Jane said confidently. 'Swedish firm buying them out, I believe.'

'Not any longer!' Jakki shot back. 'That fell through. That's why there's a problem.'

'Oh, well in that case you know more than I do,' Jane conceded. From what she'd been told by her sister-in-law, who worked for Ricky's firm, the take-over was all but completed but she wasn't going to waste time now discussing irrelevant rumours. 'Look, I want to concentrate on the match. Never know when I'll be needed.'

By now the game had been in progress for a couple of minutes and the Goal Kings were obeying their under-fire coach's orders to attack in strength. Redville, who expected to take the initiative on their own pitch, were pinned in their own half as first Lloyd and then Foggy raided down the flanks before cutting inside to feed Reuben Jones and

Davey. Reuben, however, was quickly dispossessed by a solidly-built defender and, when the same thing happened again a few moments later, Ricky displayed his annoyance.

'Come on, Reuben, get a grip – fight for the ball,' the coach sang out. Reuben gave no sign that he'd heard but a little later it was plain he'd retreated deeper into midfield as if he wanted to avoid that opponent again.

Within a minute, however, the Kings' coach and the rest of their supporters really had something to shout about. This time Lloyd managed a bit of wing wizardry in outwitting one opponent and then nutmegging another before exuberantly racing to the edge of the box. There he paused, looked up and, in text book fashion, fired in a cross with pinpoint accuracy. His target was Davey – and Davey, after taking only a couple of steps, rose majestically to head the ball down. Inexplicably his marker had dropped off at that moment and so, when the ball came down, Davey met no obstruction as he swung in almost a full circle before hitting the ball on the volley with his left foot.

To the astonishment of practically everyone who saw the shot, the ball rocketed into the roof of the net with the motionless goalkeeper powerless to do anything to stop it.

'Great goal, great goal!' Jane yelled, clapping with her hands high above her head. So far as she could remember it was the best goal she'd ever seen from a Kings' player. Her nearest companions couldn't applaud in the same way because they were still clutching their umbrellas. But they called out their congratulations before Serena pointed out, 'You saw, didn't you, that my Lloyd made that goal? Bet old Ricky doesn't recognize it, though.'

Davey was in heaven. He had no doubt at all that it was his best goal and what made it even better was that it was scored in front of Greg Kingston. As he escaped from the ecstatic clutches of his team-mates he glanced across at the Redville coach. He, though, was deep in conversation with one of his subs and taking no notice of the celebrations.

'Just the start we needed,' exclaimed Ricky, stating the obvious. But then, he needed that tonic, too. 'Now we've got to get another, quick. Redville are a big side, they'll have plenty of stamina. Bound to come back at us later.'

Davey guessed he'd be a marked man now and already he'd seen the angry stares from Ollie the boy he remembered he'd replaced during his trial with Redville. There was no mistaking Ollie's battered nose and when, a little later, they found themselves side by side in midfield, Ollie snapped, 'I'll get you, you'll suffer, mate, you'll see!'

'What?' Davey replied but was too late because Ollie had already back-pedalled out of range. Surely a goal against them didn't turn all the Rangers into a bunch of thugs? When he'd been with them he'd been impressed by some silky passing skills, especially by their red-haired, long-armed midfielder, so they hardly needed to resort to violence to win matches. The warning, though, had been explicit, so he'd have to be doubly on his guard for the remainder of the match.

Ricky's demand for a second goal seemed to be unheeded as attacking moves from the Kings quickly broke down. Once again he identified the culprit as Reuben Jones and when the boy with the fair hair sliced an intended pass to Lloyd the coach exploded.

'Get a grip, Reuben! Concentrate, think what you're doing!'

Then he turned to Jane, a few yards away, and said in a normal voice, 'His trouble is he has only one foot. Just uses the right to stand on. That's no good.'

'Give him time, Ricky,' Jane murmured. 'I'm sure he'll be fine when he fits in. This is only his second match, remember.'

Serena Colmer, who'd heard Ricky's original remark, turned to Jakki and said, loud enough for anyone to hear, 'Well, if Reuben's got a big fault like only using one foot it should be corrected on the training ground. But the coach isn't there long enough to do that these days. Half an hour, that's all the time he gave them on Tuesday, I hear.'

Ricky turned as if to answer that charge but then, thinking better of it, watched the game instead. Jane was in a dilemma: she felt Serena's criticism was valid but out of loyalty to Ricky she couldn't say so publicly. Later, though, it was something she ought to take up with him. He might think the reason she was defending Reuben was that she was the one who'd introduced the boy to the team. On the other hand, he wasn't playing up to his normal high standards. So was there a particular reason why he wasn't getting on well with his team-mates? Perhaps Dominic might know something.

Worse was to come as Redville grabbed an equalizer just when it seemed that the Kings had ridden out the storm of attacking that had naturally followed their own wonderful strike. When Kieren ventured too far upfield in pursuit of a clearance he left a gap in defence that the home side was quick to exploit. The red-haired playmaker slid another of his precise passes into the path of a team-mate who cleverly rounded Joe Parbold. For once the Rock was left floundering and then the Kings' captain was far too slow to spot the danger. Danny was well off his line and thus poorly placed to deal with what looked like a speculative lob. In fact, it was as accurate as could be. For the Redville midfielder had succeeded in floating the ball high over Danny's head before it dropped unerringly into the empty net.

Danny looked desolate, deservingly so. Ricky was speechless – temporarily. Then, as the goalkeeper retrieved the ball forlornly from the net, the coach turned and glared at Jakki Kelly.

'Have you been telling Kieren to be more adventurous? That's where the trouble started, because he was out of position.'

Jakki raised her eyebrows. There was a time when she was one of Ricky's supporters. Now she was eager to see the back of him. 'No,' she replied calmly. 'That's your job, Ricky. But you don't seem to be very good at organizing a defence, do you? I mean, what was Danny doing, standing so far out as that?'

Ricky, though, was no longer listening. He was issuing rapid instructions to his players, including one to Kieren to stay put, to maintain the line of defence. Reuben escaped censure this time but poor old Joe was told to improve his concentration. Jane listened without comment but she believed it really didn't help players to be shouted at in front of everyone else. There was a time when

Ricky, too, was cautious about making public criticisms; lately, though, he had become much more vocal. What the reason for that might be she wasn't sure but she thought she knew.

The players given fresh orders acknowledged them with nods or stony expressions but there was no immediate improvement in the Kings' play. Redville, inspired by their equalizer, inevitably charged forward again, encouraged loudly by Greg Kingston. Davey, completely unemployed at present, wondered again whether he'd made the right choice. His goal would quickly be forgotten if the Kings lost this match; there'd be changes and probably Ricky would redouble his efforts to get Alex back into the side. If that happened, then Davey sensed that the best he could hope for would be a place on the bench. If he were to tell the truth then Ricky would probably admit he didn't rate Davey Stroud as a striker. He was yet another man who thought that lack of height was a serious deficiency and couldn't be overcome. In spite of all his hard work in the gym and on the training pitch to solve the problem

Davey would be ignored when a taller player was available. Moreover, the coach probably would never forgive him for having a trial with Redville Rangers.

Then, just as Davey was imagining the worst possible scenario for himself, the ball ricocheted towards him from a scramble for possession just inside the Rangers' half. He had to move only a step to trap the ball and then twist to his left to attack down that flank. Foggy, unfortunately, was in no position to receive a pass and hadn't even broken into a jog to get into a challenging position. So Davey had to go on a solo run.

'Go on, son, keep going! Don't stop now!' he heard his coach yelling. It was all the encouragement Davey needed because he couldn't remember the last time Ricky had called to him like that. Surprisingly, the Redville defence was either back-pedalling or backing-off so Davey had plenty of room to work in; all the same, he needed support. Out of the corner of his eye he could see that Lloyd was arriving ahead of Foggy who wasn't moving with his usual freedom after taking a knock on the ankle minutes earlier.

Davey, thinking tactically, slowed and then paused before deciding on his next move. That hesitation was fatal. Ollie, who'd been chasing after him madly, made no attempt to pull out of a collision.

As Davey collapsed his opponent fell on him, his right boot driving hard into Davey's left leg, just below the knee. Ollie knew instinctively what the ref's decision would be and so, as he scrambled to his feet, he held out a hand to Davey, an offer to help that the official must surely interpret as an apology for the 'accident'.

Even with genuine support Davey was in no state to rise because the pain in his leg was too fierce. His face contorted, he simply lay prone, clutching the injury until Jane Allenby arrived at his side to try to take the pain away. The ref, who wasn't taken in by Ollie's gesture of contrition, already had his notebook out and was telling the offender: 'You deserve to be sent off for that, you really do. But there won't be a second warning, son. Another offence of any kind and you're off this pitch faster than a Formula One start!'

Jane's fingers were exploring Davey's calf

and she was surprised how firm it was. Boys of his age weren't usually quite so muscular in that area.

'I'm sure you're going to be all right because you've got such strong legs,' she told him in a reassuring fashion. 'How have you built up such muscles?'

'In the gym,' he gasped. 'Weight-training – I want to be able to jump high.'

'Well, you can certainly do that, Davey. Wonderful goal you scored.' Her fingers were now helping to stroke away the tenderness of the kick from Ollie's boot. Then she applied the pain-killing spray before a final massage. She watched the tears fade away and the brightness return to his quite start-lingly blue eyes. 'How d'you feel now?' she added, giving him a hand to help him to his feet.

Predictably, he staggered a little and when he started to walk she could tell her treatment hadn't been completely effective. Probably he really needed a rest before running again.

'I'll be OK,' he muttered, biting his upper lip. 'It's not so bad now.'

'Sure you wouldn't like to come off for a

few minutes? It's nearly half-time.'

'No, I'll be fine,' he muttered unconvincingly. 'If I'm not on the pitch I can't score goals. That's my job.'

'I know, but –'

'You've got to be in the right place at the right time,' Davey added. 'That proves you have the instincts of a real striker. The German manager said that last week.'

Jane was impressed that he could talk so rationally when she was sure he was still suffering badly from that horrendous tackle. It underlined just how determined he was to hold on to his new role now that Alex was missing. She turned to see whether Ricky was in earshot and whether he wanted a word with the Kings' goal-scorer. The coach, however, was in conversation further along the touch-line with Taylor Hill. Larry, though, was still on the bench, metaphorically speaking, as the Redville ground didn't provide seats of any kind for anyone.

'Well, just signal if the pain comes back,' she told Davey who nodded as he moved away, plainly trying to avoid any suggestion of a limp.

The free kick had come to nothing and the Kings seemed to have lost their attacking initiative. When the half-time whistle sounded it was Rangers who were dominating again and they'd've taken the lead but for a splendid save by Danny who somehow got fingertips to a ball that seemed certain to end up in the corner of the net. Joe displayed his defensive skills to hook the ball away from a poor header by Tree when the corner kick was taken but the next corner was wasted when the kicker misdirected the ball over the line.

'I don't know what's got into you but you're a shadow of the team you were last season,' Ricky told them as the boys assembled under a chestnut tree, the 'garden shed' dressing-room not being available at half-time as it was locked for security reasons, according to one knowledgeable spectator interrogated by Josh's mother, Karen Rowley, who had turned up late. 'Some of you are simply going through the motions instead of getting stuck in. What's happened to your commitment?'

Of course, nobody said a word in reply and

most of the players stared stonily at the ground. Then, as if to break the embarrassed silence, Foggy spoke up.

'I'd play like a maniac but I got kicked by that red-haired slinker who's supposed to be their midfield general or whatever he calls himself. But I played on, didn't collapse just to get loads of sympathy.' He shot a glance at Davey but Davey wasn't really listening. He was still massaging his leg muscles.

Ricky was in no mood to listen to hard-luck stories. 'Marc, if you're saying you're not fit enough to play on then I'll take you off now. I'm sick of feeble excuses.' He swung round to look at Davey. 'And what about you, are you packing it in as well? Why did I have the idea that the Goal Kings were the sort of players who don't recognize a pain barrier? Was it only last season that people could put up with the odd knock, the odd bruise!'

Jane, noting the harshness in his tone, moved closer and took him by the elbow to draw him away from the boys for a moment. 'Ricky, don't be too hard on them,' she advised. 'I think they're down enough as it is. They *know* things are going badly.'

He shot her a glance and then nodded. 'You're probably right, Jane. It's just that, well, I'm so disappointed in them.'

'Of course,' she agreed, 'we all are. But I'm also sure Davey's not a malingerer. I've checked his injury and he really did take a fearsome kick in his calf. He's bound to be sore. I don't think Davey's the sort of boy to give in to anything less. He's desperate to score goals for us. Oh, and Foggy's much the same.' She paused and then added quietly, 'In fact, they're both eager to take Alex's place permanently, if it's available.'

'Oh, I think you can take that as read,' he conceded. 'I'm sure that Alex and the rest of us are going down separate paths. OK, I'll try to cheer 'em up while there's still time.'

He was too late. The ref, aware that the pitch was deteriorating fast in the unceasing rain, wanted the game to resume without further delay. As the boys trooped back to their positions for the kick-off Jane managed a word with Davey.

'Is your leg any better?'

He shrugged. 'Well, it's no worse. I know the Boss thinks I'm making it up but, honest,

I'm not. I'm going to get another goal if it – it *kills* me!'

'Don't go that far!' she smiled. 'Play as long as you can but signal me if it gets worse again.'

The moment the game was flowing again Taylor Hill, having waited until Ricky was on his own, buttonholed him. 'I heard the chat about the injuries. So why aren't you taking one of 'em off and putting on a fully-fit striker? I mean, that must be the answer to our problem of not getting enough goals.'

Ricky was tempted to make a sarcastic remark because, of course, he knew exactly what Mr Hill was getting at; but he realized just in time that there was nothing to be gained by antagonizing a Kings' supporter. 'Might just do that before long,' he replied mildly.

'Oh, er, good,' Mr Hill murmured, having anticipated a very different answer. 'Lawrence here never misses a day's schooling, never seems to get knocked about at sport. Fitness is a way of life for our family, I've got to admit it. And we all eat the right food!'

'*Dad*,' Larry, embarrassed by this blatant bid for a substitution, hissed between clenched teeth. He was as keen as any sub could be to get into the action but he knew that Ricky Todd wasn't the sort of coach who could be manipulated by a parent.

Neither of them would ever know how Ricky Todd might have dealt with that situation because, at that moment, the mobile phone rang in the coach's pocket. 'Yes?' he said crisply after putting it to his ear. Because the Hills were so close they could hear every word Ricky uttered and it was obvious this wasn't a casual, social call. An emergency of some kind needed his attention wherever it was happening. 'Be with you in ten minutes,' were his final words into the phone.

'Sorry about this,' he said to Jane as he went to stand beside her near the half-way line. 'But I've got to leave now – the Company take-over bid seems to have reached a critical point and I'm needed at the office. Right now. So, I've got to leave you in charge. Just do as you think fit. You know the boys as well as I do.'

Jane, startled, asked, 'But what about

putting subs on and tactics like that?'

'Whatever's needed, you do it, Jane. I won't be back before the final whistle so I'm afraid you'll have to pick up the pieces if we lose. Or take the glory if we win!' He managed a wan smile. 'Maybe this is what they need, a change of coach. Good luck, anyway.'

7 Early Finish

Even as Ricky hurried away towards his car, Redville struck again to take the lead for the first time in the match. Several Kings' supporters who saw him depart then concluded that was why he went.

Rangers had won a throw-in almost opposite the Rodale penalty area and when their long-armed midfielder took it, the ball was tapped back to him immediately. Without seeming to take any aim he hit a prodigious kick into the box although none of his strikers could hope to reach it. That didn't matter. For when the ball bounced upwards again off a rare firm patch of ground Kieren and Tree both rose to head it clear. Kieren was the unlucky one. For as the defenders collided in their eagerness to get to the ball it skimmed off Kieren's head and spun towards the net. Danny made a despairing dive to try to reach it but his fingers weren't long enough to get a touch before the ball flicked against the inside of the post and fell into the rigging.

Kieren and Tree were still picking themselves up abjectly as Jane yelled, 'It only needed one of you to clear it! Why didn't you call out to claim it?'

It hadn't registered with any of the players yet that Ricky had gone and Jane was now in charge. So none of them reacted, apart from Dominic, who wasn't used to hearing his mum utter public criticisms. Dominic agreed with her: the Kings had given away the softest of goals and now they were losing. Every Rodale fan was entitled to be upset.

Jakki Kelly was especially upset on Kieren's behalf. 'Just forget it, Kier, it couldn't be helped,' she called. Kieren, lost in misery, didn't hear her. He was imagining what Mr Todd would say if the Kings lost this match because of his dreadful error.

Danny, for one, wasn't going to let the setback get him down. 'Come on, boys, let's hit back, let's get a winner. Kings rule!'

Rangers, inevitably, wanted to capitalize on

the situation and score again to put the issue beyond doubt. Greg Kingston was urging them to still more frantic endeavour. He'd seen Ricky Todd's departure and believed the man was walking out on his team. Perhaps it was a habit of the Kings to collapse when they'd gone behind and their coach couldn't bring himself to witness such a surrender.

'You've got them on the run, you Reds, so keep hitting 'em,' he urged.

Ollie took the words literally. The moment Davey gained possession he charged in, determined to bring him down. For once, though, luck was on Davey's side. Ollie missed his target on the greasy turf, fell awkwardly and twisted his own knee. While play was held up for him to receive attention Davey watched the Rangers' physio at work. Ollie was plainly in pain but at last managed to get to his feet.

'Why d'you keep attacking me?' Davey enquired mildly, sensing there was nothing to be gained by violent words.

'I don't get into the team regularly, that's why, and it's all because of you,' was Ollie's totally unexpected reply. 'Greg Kingston says

I'm not as good as you. So I want to prove I *am* better than you!'

Davey, quickly overcoming his amazement, replied, 'He's just winding you up! That's what coaches do.'

That exchange proved to be something of a tonic for Davey and when next he picked up a pass he exploited his pace and turning skills to outwit two defenders and hurtle towards the byline. His injury still bothered him but he didn't forget Greg Kingston's advice that top strikers should find a way to overcome the pain barrier. If he could get a second goal today he ought to be able to clinch his place in the side whatever happened with Alex. Now, turning and shielding the ball, he looked for support. 'Fogs!' he yelled as Marc Thrale came into the box. Hitting a sharp pass to the boy with the voice Davey darted inside for a one-two.

Foggy, however, didn't foresee Davey's plan and simply hit the ball as hard as he could and succeeded only in ballooning it over the bar. It had been a clear-cut chance and Jane shook her head in despair as did most of the Kings' supporters.

Davey was reaching down to rub his calf when he remembered his decision never to show discomfort because that only heartened the opposition. So, deliberately bouncing on his toes, he trotted back towards the centre, still buoyed by Ollie's disclosure of Kingston's rating of his skills, confirmed, of course, by the coach's phone call.

As the game continued almost as drearily as the still falling rain, Taylor Hill sidled up to the new temporary Kings' coach. 'Listen, I heard what Ricky told you. So it's about time you put my boy on. I mean, Davey's still carrying an injury and that Marc is useless. Well, he is today. You've got to make changes if we're ever going to get back into this game, salvage a point, that sort of thing.'

Jane, who'd been on the verge of doing exactly that, hesitated. If she accepted Mr Hill's advice would that demonstrate that she didn't have a mind of her own and could be manipulated by anyone with a personal ambition to fulfil? On the other hand, time really was running out if the Kings were to score an equalizer.

'We're on the same wavelength,' she said,

smiling broadly. After all, honesty had to come first. 'Larry, time to get out of your track-suit and ready for action. A couple of warm-up sprints first, I think.'

Larry beamed. Above medium height with broad shoulders and dark hair flattened over a high forehead, he had always believed he would score goals for any team. But at least two teachers had told him he looked 'too soft' to be an aggressive striker and they'd stuck him in midfield, not even trusting him as a back-line defender.

'Good thinking,' Taylor Hill congratulated Jane. 'We'll see a difference when Lawrence gets on the pitch.'

Foggy was the player to be replaced. For some reason she couldn't quite fathom he had lost his touch; perhaps he was simply too anxious to please in Alex's absence. That was close to the truth but Foggy was always annoyed when someone else scored for the Kings and he didn't. His jealousy now extended to Davey Stroud who, Foggy suspected, had somehow become a favourite of Mrs Allenby's. When she signalled vigorously to come off he was sure of it. For a few moments he wondered whether to defy her and stay on the pitch. If he displayed enough determination, he guessed, she might abandon the intended substitution. Then his courage deserted him and, mulishly, he came off.

'You took your time,' she said, though not waspishly.

'Where's the Boss?' Foggy wanted to know. 'He's the one who does the subs.'

'I'm the Boss now,' Jane told him in words she hadn't planned to use. But then it occurred to her that she was. 'I'm giving Larry a run out, we need fresh legs in these sticky conditions. Did you get a knock earlier on?'

'Er, yeah, but I thought I could run it off,' replied Foggy, thinking quickly now and pleased to have a ready excuse for his substitution when he talked to team-mates later.

Larry, ordered up front where he was to chase anything that hinted at a chance of a goal, bounded into action. His leap for a loose ball from a clearance kick by Danny provided him with an opportunity to run at the

Rangers' defence. Although he lacked Davey's electric acceleration he could control the ball at speed and was difficult to dispossess because he seemed to be all arms and elbows and knees. It was only when he was sandwiched between central defenders and slipped on the mud of midfield that he lost the ball. However, he had won a free kick. Wiping the earth off his white shorts and hooped socks but displaying no irritation at his treatment, he trotted forward as Reuben Jones lined up the kick about five metres outside the box.

'Back, Back, BACK!' Mr Kingston was shrieking at his defence. With only two minutes of the match remaining he would be apoplectic if his team conceded a goal now. They deserved to win – and they were going to win! It crossed his mind that it might be a neat tactical ploy to make a substitution now while Rodale were preparing the kick. At the same time, he didn't think any of his players was too tired to continue and none deserved to be replaced. So, to his later regret, he took no action.

As always, Josh raced forward to be

involved. His height could trouble any defence and he wanted it to work for him now. If the ball came his way and he got his header right then he could get the equalizer. He would be the hero. That, above all, was what he wanted.

Reuben, however, was never predictable. His contact with Larry Hill had been minimal in training but he supposed the new attacker would be able to head the ball; and, what's more, Larry had taken up a position by the near post as if he hoped for a low cross. With unerring accuracy Reuben floated the ball in and Larry surprised everyone by heading it backwards as he rose above his marker. Davey seized his chance and hurled himself forward to bundle the ball into the net. But it was he who ended up in the net as two defenders desperately, and literally, fell on him to try to avert disaster.

As Davey, luckily unharmed, got to his feet the boys who'd sandwiched him turned, arms aloft, claiming innocence. For, like everyone else, they'd heard the shrill whistle and guessed it meant a penalty. Davey, seeing the ref's pointing finger, grabbed the ball and hugged it against his chest. He was the victim and he was going to exact revenge. It didn't matter to him who normally took penalties for the Kings, Davey Stroud was taking this one.

Danny, as skipper, had the right to say who should be the penalty taker but he wasn't going to argue: even from the edge of his own area he could sense Davey's determination. Jane knew she shouldn't interfere; if things went wrong, well, there would be an inquest later. All the same, she wished that Ricky had been present to give his opinion of what should happen. For this one kick would almost certainly determine the result of the match.

'I ought to be taking it. I'd score, no danger,' Foggy was muttering beside Jane.

'My Lawrence is good on penalty kicks,' murmured Taylor Hill, also running true to form.

'Best of luck, Davey,' said Josh, patting his team-mate on the shoulder before leaving the box.

Davey had no doubts whatsoever that he would score. Taking only a couple of paces he turned, ran in, hit the ball as hard as he knew how and watched it flash into the roof of the net, giving the keeper no earthly chance of getting even a finger to it.

'Yes!' he and half of his team exulted.

Jane joined in the applause but called warningly, 'Don't get over-excited! Don't give it away now, Kings!'

They didn't. The defence proved impenetrable when Redville desperately tried to score the winner and Danny thoughtfully wasted precious seconds when the ball was in his hands. Greg Kingston did his best to roar his team on with claims that, 'You'll feel robbed if we only draw!' But the score was still 2–2 at the final whistle.

'We should've won, not drawn. But then I suppose we might easily have lost,' Mr Hill summed it up. 'Might have been different if my lad had been on from the start. You can see he knows a trick or two, can't you? That back-header was a dream.'

'Yes, Mr Hill, I'll bear that in mind for the future,' Jane replied diplomatically. She couldn't deny that the substitution had worked and she could claim some credit for it. Of course, no doubt Ricky Todd would have his own ideas about that because it was he who'd included Larry in the squad.

Davey was glowing. In spite of the soreness in his calf and the ache in his side where he'd been elbowed late in the game, he believed it had been a brilliant game for him. Scorer of the Kings' two goals, he must surely keep his place for the next match. Danny, ever enthusiastic, gave him an extra hug as they left the pitch and excitedly proclaimed, 'We pulled it back. Knew we would. And it's thanks to you, Davey boy!' That was generous because Danny's own contribution had been majestic for much of the match.

Ironically, the rain had stopped now but all the players were glad to get into and then out of the wooden shed as fast as possible. Jane accompanied them for a few moments to explain that Ricky Todd had been called away but she knew he'd be as pleased as she was by their fight back. It had, she said, been a real team effort. None of the players made much of a response apart from a grin or a raised thumb. Dominic hoped his mum wasn't going to stay around too long because he was as eager as anyone to get home.

'Well done, you Kings!' she said in farewell before saving a last word for Reuben. 'That was a wonderful free kick. It saved the game for us, Reuben.'

He looked surprised and then, as he started to change out of his soaked kit, he allowed himself one of his rare smiles.

Jane looked round for Jakki and Serena as she made her way to her car but they had vanished. She just hoped the draw had cheered them up a bit.

It was late that evening when the phone rang in the Allenby household and Ken declined to take the call. 'Bound to be for you,' he told his wife. 'Only hospitals and patients about to give birth ring at this hour.'

'But none of my patients is anywhere near her time at present,' Jane pointed out. 'And I've had a really long day. *And* I coped with all the trauma of the Kings' game. Perhaps it'll stop ringing in a moment. Wrong number, I guess.'

It didn't stop and so Jane, with a sigh of exasperation, picked up the receiver. 'Oh,

Ricky,' she said moments later. 'Didn't expect you to be ringing at this time.'

Ken, knowing this conversation would be all about football, returned to the novel he was reading. But the call proved to be much shorter than expected and Jane said very little apart from, 'Really?' and, 'Well, I am sorry' and then, right at the end, 'So you're absolutely sure, Ricky? No possibility of a change of mind? All right, well, thanks for the vote of confidence. I just hope everybody else feels the same. Right, bye then.'

Ken looked up from his book. 'So, what was all that about?' he wanted to know. 'Sounded a bit mysterious.'

Jane made a point of sitting down on the sofa before answering. She looked, Ken thought, rather stunned. 'Nothing mysterious about it. Very straightforward, really. Ricky Todd's packed it in as coach and he's asked me to take over. Says everyone he's talked to thinks I'm the obvious candidate to succeed him. Can hardly believe it.'

Ken's eyebrows went up. 'But why's he giving up? Thought he was – what's the word? – committed, totally committed, to the Kings.'

'He was, but he's having a bad time with supporters and some of the team – Alex, for a start. But also his business life is hectic with this take-over. Seems there's another foreign company wants the factory. German, this time. That's why he had to leave the game this morning. Some top German guy had arrived in London and Ricky was needed. He says things could get still more complicated. Anyway, the point is that football's out for him for the present.'

'You accepted the invitation, then?'

'Well, yes. I mean, I feel honoured. And I do have ideas that may turn things round for us. Ricky's never bothered much with our defence, you know. Attack was everything to him.'

'What about Dominic, though? How's he going to cope with his mum being his boss at football?'

'Oh, I don't see a problem there, Ken. Dominic's used to me being on the touch-line. He knows the rest of the squad accept me as the physio. They know I *care* about their football.'

'Well, that's all right, then,' said Ken,

though he didn't sound convinced.

'Oh, there's no way I'm going to fall out with my own son, as Ricky's done,' Jane went on. 'Dominic and I have always got on, haven't we? All three of us have. No, Dominic will be the least of my problems.'

Ken nodded. 'So the phone call *was* about a baby, after all.'

Jane frowned. 'I don't follow.'

Her husband grinned. 'The Goal Kings are now *your* baby! The difference here is that you're not just restricted to delivering them. You've got to help them grow up!'

'Oh, very good, Ken!' She paused. 'But you're right, I've got to agree. The really hard work begins now. And it's all down to me.'

'Are you sure you'll be able to cope? Devote enough time to this football?'

'Yes, I won't be putting in many more hours, just more thinking. I can do that any time I like. Obviously training will be extra time but lately I've been going to that, anyway, with Ricky having other things to attend to. Don't worry, darling, I won't neglect you in favour of full-time football!'

He laughed. 'Oh, I know that. We've

always had time for each other and for Dominic and our jobs. The secret of our success as a couple, isn't it?'

'Absolutely. Now I've got to find a way of achieving success for the Goal Kings. They've been on the slide long enough. We've got to start climbing, climbing to the top.'

'Well, knowing you, my love, you'll find a way. Or you'll make one.'

8 A Different Game

Just as Jane and Dominic were about to leave the house for the weekly evening training session the phone rang. 'Not again!' Jane said, annoyed at the thought of any delay. 'You get it, please, Dom. Say I'm out – I practically am!' She wished she could ignore the call altogether but it just might be an emergency. Dominic had no sooner picked up the receiver than he was holding it out to her. 'It's Kieren's mum, says it's important.'

'Jane, do you mind if I join you at training tonight?' Jakki enquired. 'I mean, I suppose I'm offering my services as a helper if you need me. Even if you don't, I just want to lend support. It's so marvellous we've got a woman coach.'

Jane's instinct was to refuse the offer because she preferred to be on her own, especially as this was the first time she'd be in charge. In some ways it would make it more difficult to have an audience even if those spectators were on her side. On the other hand, she didn't want to get off on the wrong foot by rebuffing one of the players' mums.

'Be pleased to see you, Jakki, of course I will,' she replied with as much enthusiasm as she could muster. 'When I knew it was you I feared that Kieren might be injured or ill.'

'Far from it. He's really looking forward to being coached by you. Says you'll understand him far better than Ricky did. See you presently.'

Since the weekend Jane had received a string of calls from Kings' supporters, including several of the players' mothers, all of whom had unreservedly welcomed her appointment which the committee had formally endorsed once Ricky sent in his resignation. She'd been surprised how many of them said that Ricky either didn't take much interest in certain players or failed to get the best out of them. Serena Colmer, for instance, claimed that Ricky had never given Lloyd any encouragement so she was sure

Jane would 'look after him'. Remarkably, nobody at all seemed to regret Ricky's departure. But then, he hadn't led the team to any triumphs in Cups or Championships: quite the reverse, for the team was still without a win in the current season. These days, Jane recognized, teams were judged – and so were their coaches, therefore – on the silverware they collected. It was a daunting thought that she herself would suffer the same scrutiny in the months to come.

'Mum, you're not going to pick on me during this training, are you?' Dominic asked just before they reached the car-park of the leisure centre where they used the all-weather pitch.

'Of course not. Why on earth would I do that?' She wasn't entirely surprised by the question because her only son had said very little to her about the Kings since the news of her new role became public. She guessed he was worrying about it but she didn't want to ask him what his team-mates were saying. Above all, she must never let him think she wanted anything from him other than his normal contribution to the team's play. She didn't need a spy in the dressing-room and she'd already emphasized that to him.

'But you won't ignore me, either, will you?' he asked.

'Of course I won't! I shall treat you just like the rest of the boys. I know it's going to be a bit difficult at first, Dom, but you'll soon get used to it. All of you will. Just remember Alex: he coped all right when his dad was in charge, didn't he?'

'Only sometimes. Then he walked out, didn't he? That was because everything got so awful. Hope I never have to do the same!'

Then he hopped out of the car and ran across to join some of the other players who were already kicking a ball about on the edge of the pitch. Before Jane could reflect on that unexpected remark she was hailed by Jakki who was dashing towards her, wreathed in smiles. Jane always thought of Jakki as really her opposite number because she was small and blonde and very outgoing and Jane could see what an impression she must have made when she was lead singer in a rock band before her marriage to Kieren's dad, Clark.

'Just wanted you to know we all wish you

lots of luck and that we're right behind you,' she gushed, throwing her arms around Jane and giving her a kiss and a hug.

'Same from me, Coach, best of luck,' said Kieren, holding out his hand. That rather formal gesture from one of her players was every bit as surprising as Jakki's warmth and Jane was touched. When she'd accepted Ricky's offer she'd feared that some of the other women involved with the Kings might not favour a female coach and that the boys themselves wouldn't want her, perhaps for a variety of reasons. So far, though, everyone she'd met or heard from had welcomed her appointment.

'Well, thanks, I'm really grateful for your support,' she told them. 'Please don't give up on me if things don't go right immediately. Remember, I'm a novice at this job. I've got to learn to put things over in the right way so that we make progress.'

'You'll make it, Jane, I know you will,' said Jakki reassuringly. 'And don't forget that I'm here to help whenever you need me.'

Moments later Jane had summoned the players to what she said was her first 'official' meeting as their new coach. 'I'm not going to say a lot because it would be a waste of time when we need to get down to serious training this evening,' she began as they stood in a semicircle around her at the side of the pitch. 'I just want you to know that although some things are bound to change because I'm a different person from Mr Todd, many things will stay the same. The most important thing for you to know is that you'll all be treated equally. Everyone will be given his chance to show what he can do *for the team*. That's the vital ingredient in all we're striving for, the team, the Goal Kings. No one is bigger than the team. We're here to play for each other, for the team. Any personal ambition must take second place to the team's ambitions to win Cups and Championships. Anyone disagree?'

She had sensed that every eye was on her but now she glanced round to see reactions. Some shook their heads but most remained stone-faced. The coach was wearing a very serious expression and they felt they had to respond in the same way.

'Good,' she resumed, smiling brightly

again. 'I'm delighted to see that every member of the squad has turned up tonight. That must mean you're all on my side and want to be in the team. Now, I can imagine that one thing might worry you: my presence in the dressing-room. Well, it mustn't. We're not going to let any silly little embarrassments come between us. I treat your injuries so you're already used to me. I'll need to talk to you all as a team at regular intervals so the dressing-room is likely to be the most convenient place.

'OK, just one other important thing: the past is the past. We're starting afresh from this moment and so what happened last Sunday or last month or last season is no longer relevant. It's what we do now and in the future that we're concerned with. Any old jealousies or resentments or what somebody else said or did, they're yesterday. Yesterday is *dead*. We're alive and looking forward to tomorrow.'

At that point Jakki Kelly couldn't restrain herself from applauding. Jane rather wished she hadn't but then recognized that she was receiving support, not facing opposition. So she nodded a smile at Jakki and Serena and Karen Rowley who had just arrived.

'Right, that's it, except to say that I'm not inviting you to ask me any questions just now,' she concluded. 'I'm sure you *do* want to ask about something but I'd rather you took time to think things over. Then, when we get together before the next match, you can raise any points you wish. I'll probably have talked to you individually before then, anyway. But if you're *desperate* about something that's really important to you, well, you can always phone me. I'll make time for you, I promise.'

After that, they got down to some serious training. She split the squad into two groups of eight: one to try out a new game to improve heading skills, the other to practise a dribbling-and-shooting-on-the-run exercise. For the latter she put Danny, as skipper, in charge because she felt it might be good both for his image and his authority. It had occurred to her to ask Jakki if she'd care to supervise that particular workout at the other end of the pitch but then decided it wasn't fair on Jakki, who'd be thrown in at the deep end without any warning, or on Danny, who ought to relish being elevated to a role akin to assistant coach.

She led the remainder, who included Dominic and Davey and Kieren, over to the penalty area and then explained that she wanted two teams of four. The idea of this game was that the ball should be headed whenever possible and never kicked. The attacking team must throw the ball to each other or in some way pass it on with the hand with the objective of heading it into the net for a goal, and goals could *only* be headed. The defenders could use both hands to save shots but must throw the ball out as far as possible for the attackers to regain possession and build up another attack. The zone to be used was only a little deeper than the penalty area and so there should be plenty of scoring opportunities.

'Sometimes you're going to have to throw yourself at the ball for a low-level header so you need to keep your wits about you – and be brave,' she pointed out.

The sheer novelty of the game took the players by surprise and initially they were inclined to kick the ball when they should have been knocking it on with their hand or attempting a pass with an upward, looping header. Once they'd got the hang of it, though, their laughter and whoops of excitement when a goal was scored showed how much they were enjoying it. After less than ten minutes she gave the players a breather before switching them round so that the original attackers were now the defence.

'You really can get high when you jump, can't you?' she remarked to Davey in the interval. 'Very impressive for –'

'–someone of my size!' Davey completed her sentence correctly with a grin. 'I work on it. Weight training and running up and down stairs carrying weights, that sort of thing. It all helps strengthen important muscles.'

She nodded. 'I can tell. Davey, you were brilliant against Redville and I admire the way you never flinched in spite of a painful injury. You're exactly what I need in my team.'

'Thanks, Coach,' he murmured. Then, just as she was registering that the boys had obviously decided what they were going to call her, Davey added softly, 'I want to be in your team because you won't walk out on us, will you? Women don't walk out, that's what my mum said. I mean, my dad walked out on us and then Mr Todd walked out on the Kings, didn't he? My dad came back but I like things to stay the same all the time.'

She put her arm round his shoulders and hugged him, hoping none of the others would see that as some sort of favouritism. 'Davey, that's my aim, too. I want the players to stay the same and our game to get better. I can promise you, the Kings and I have a long way to go together.'

So far Dominic had given no sign that he was troubled by her role as coach instead of just being their physio and he was playing as wholeheartedly as he usually did in training sessions. He even scored with a particularly clever sideways header to overcome sandwich-style marking. So she clapped vigorously, 'Well done, Dominic!'

At the other end of the pitch Danny was instinctively following her lead, singing out praise when anyone fired in a good shot or put the ball into the net past him or the other stand-in goalie, Gareth Kingstree. Gareth's family had moved to Rodale during the previous season and so far he hadn't established a place in the team although he always said he was happy to play anywhere. It was one of the squad's jokes that Gareth had only been invited to join them because his name included the word 'Kings'. He claimed that proved he was a natural for the side.

Jane watched in silence for a few minutes before bringing that exercise to an end with one blast of her referee's whistle. It was plain to her that one or two players had put in extra effort because they saw that she was observing them but she couldn't fault them for that; it was natural for any player to want to impress the coach, especially when that coach was so new.

'OK,' she announced after summoning the entire squad together. 'We'll have a break for a couple of minutes and then practise defending at corners and free kicks. I think we're not always taking up the best positions, we're not always sure who we should be marking. We really need to rectify that. Also, we need to *talk* to each other more. D'you know what I mean by that?'

If they did they weren't going to admit it; and if they didn't they weren't going to reveal their ignorance. Jane was about to ask a further question when it suddenly occurred to her that their lack of response almost certainly meant they didn't feel they could trust her yet. She was still a completely unknown quantity to them – as a coach. Moreover, in their experience, a coach *told* them what to do: he, or she, didn't ask for opinions very often. Well, in time they'd find she *wanted* to hear their views, their hopes and ambitions. For the present, though, she must simply lead them.

'Well, it's just this: no one has eyes in the back of his head. So when danger threatens behind us it helps enormously if somebody calls, "Look out!" or, "Behind you!" or something like that. We've had the situation, too, where two players have gone for the same ball – collided – and lost it. If one had called, "My ball!" the other would have had time to pull out, to drop back or mark an opponent. So when you think it might be helpful, use your voice. *Communicate*. OK now?'

This time they managed to indicate their agreement in a variety of ways with one or two shouting 'Yes!' as loudly as possible to show they really could use their voices; and that caused a burst of laughter.

'Good! Your sense of humour shows you must be enjoying yourselves,' she told them with the warmest smile. 'And that's always good for team spirit.'

Once again she soon switched players around, turning attackers into defenders and midfielders into wingers as she took them through a variety of set-pieces. She knew what most of them were capable of in their regular roles in the team but she was keen to see how they might be stretched. For some time it had been her impression that several of the squad had great potential but had been playing well short of it under Ricky Todd's rule. For some reason they hadn't displayed the range of abilities she'd already witnessed in them tonight. Could it be that they'd been *afraid* of Ricky? Had they been afraid of offending him in some way and thus risked being dropped from the team? Probably she'd never know the answer to that question. Well, it must *never* happen in the future: under her leadership the players must always feel she was on their side, never against them.

When the session was over she made a point of thanking them all for their hard work and enthusiasm, adding that she hoped they'd enjoyed themselves. 'And that's it until our match on Sunday. We're going to win that one and we're going to keep winning for the rest of the season. So, boys, we've all got a lot to look forward to. See you all on Sunday.'

There was just one player she wanted a word with before they all departed: Reuben. She took him to one side and said quietly, 'Reuben, I've been thinking about your place in the team and your particular skills. I –'

'Oh, I know,' he interrupted, managing to sound both irritated and resigned at the same time. 'You want me to use my right foot more, don't you? You think I'm not performing properly because I'm one-footed.'

She was astonished. 'Nothing of the sort! Quite the reverse. I want you to make still more use of your left-foot skills. They're marvellous. I think that if anyone's got a talent then it should be employed as much as possible. Make the most of it, that's my motto. But why did you say that?'

'Oh, all the coaches I've met think I should use the right just as much as the left,' he said, looking a little brighter. 'Mr Todd was another of them. Said he'd leave me out if I didn't improve. Thought you'd be the same.'

'I'd no idea Mr Todd said that. Reuben, my approach is entirely different. I saw tonight that you have more speed than I'd imagined. I want to exploit that. I want you playing just behind the strikers, setting up chances for them but also going forward and scoring goals when the opening's there. How d'you feel about that?'

'Yeah, I'd like that, I really would.' By now he was positively beaming. 'Thanks, Mrs Allenby.'

'Reuben, I'm confident the Kings are going to enjoy lots of success and you're going to make one of the biggest contributions to that,' she said as she patted him on the back and wished him good night.

Danny walked off the pitch with Larry and

163

asked him what he thought about the new coach.

'Well, brilliant. I mean, she put me on against Redville, didn't she, and now she's given me lots to do in training,' was the enthusiastic response. 'Ricky Todd didn't have any faith in me. Just wanted to stick with his own son, didn't he? How about you, *Skipper*?'

'Oh yeah, I'm in favour. I know he didn't pick you much, Larry, but Ricky really only thought about the attack. He didn't have much time for the defence, except to blame us if things went wrong. Mrs Allenby's going to be different. And she's dead right about us not talking to each other, letting someone know when there's danger. I'm always telling my defenders to do that. Maybe they'll listen now the coach says it!'

Foggy, however, was one player who wasn't convinced the change in leadership was going to be for the better. He passed on his grumble to Lloyd Colmer though, for once, he made an effort to keep his voice down. 'She seems keen on Davey to be the main striker and now she keeps picking Larry to do things as well. I mean, neither of 'em would have been given any chance at all if I hadn't picked up an injury. If she sticks with them I might never get back into the team. That'd be a disaster for the Kings!'

'Oh, I don't know about that, Fogs. I think she's a very fair sort of person. If you keep banging in the goals in training you'll be back in the team, you'll see. She likes *fast* players, so that's why I'm practising my sprinting all the time. You ought to do the same, Fogs. Then you'd be a certainty for the team – maybe!' Lloyd's radiant smile was one of his brightest. 'Got to have a word with Dominic. See you!'

He dashed away while Foggy, beginning to limp again, made his way towards the changing-rooms.

As the Kings' squad departed from the leisure centre later, in ones and twos, Davey found himself on his own. He didn't mind that because strikers often were isolated on the pitch and, anyway, he had good memories of the weekend and this evening. The future, he felt, had never looked brighter.

'The ball's being driven in to the penalty

area by Reuben Jones and the opposition's defence is all over the place,' he told his invisible audience as he strolled along. 'Davey Stroud is closely marked. But as the ball comes over Davey gets to it first. He chests it down – he pushes it past the nearest defender – and now he has only the goalie to beat. Davey *must* score – and he does! And that's his third goal. Yet another Davey Stroud hat trick for the Goal Kings. What a player!'

If you particularly enjoy reading about football, why not try some of these other Faber children's books?

Goal Kings by Michael Hardcastle

BOOK ONE: Shoot-Out
BOOK TWO: Eye for a Goal
BOOK THREE: And Davey Must Score
BOOK FOUR: They All Count

Life in the Junior Football League can be tough. This adventure-packed series follows the dramas and excitements – on and off the pitch – in the lives of Goal Kings JFC.

Own Goal by Michael Hardcastle

Russell is passionate about football but he has a problem: he scores own goals. Then, amazingly, he discovers a footballing talent he never dared dream of.

One Kick by Michael Hardcastle

Jamie finds that all is not fair play on the field. He makes a mistake that is to haunt him for weeks and almost put a stop to his footballing career . . .

Second Chance by Michael Hardcastle

Scott is an ace striker. But when he moves to a school where soccer comes a poor second to cricket, he faces an unexpected and difficult challenge . . .

Frances Fairweather: Demon Striker!
by Derek Smith

Frances is so obsessed with football that she gets thrown out of the girls' team, and the boys' team won't have her either. Drastic measures are called for: Frances decides to become 'Frank' . . .

Faber children's books are available from most bookshops. For a complete catalogue, please write to: The Children's Marketing Department, Faber and Faber, 3 Queen Square, London WC1N 3AU.